Larry Ivkovich's speculative fiction has been published in over twenty-five online and print publications. He's been a finalist in the L. Ron Hubbard's Writers of the Future contest and was the 2010 recipient of the CZP/Rannu Fund award for fiction. Larry has a story in an upcoming anthology later this year titled *Tales from the Wood*, which features fantasy stories inspired by the music of Jethro Tull.

His four-part urban fantasy series, *The Spirit Winds Quartet*, is published by IFWG Publishing, and the first two books in his independently published science fiction series, *The Magus Star Trilogy*, are available on Amazon. Forthcoming from IFWG in 2024 is Larry's SF/Steampunk novella, *Hope's Song*.

Larry is a member of the Pittsburgh SF organization Parsec, the writing/critique group WorD, Pennsylvania Statewide Writers' Group Pennwriters, and the Pittsburgh Mindful Writers. He lives in Coraopolis, PA with his beautiful, multi-talented wife Martha and wonder cat Milo.

Larry Ivkovich Books Published by IFWG Publishing Australia

The Spirit Winds Quartet
  The Sixth Precept (Bk 1)
  Warriors of the Light (Bk 2)
  Orchus Unchained (Bk 3)
  Return of the Luminous One (Bk 4)

Hope's Song (novella)

Hope's Song

by
Larry Ivkovich

Hope's Song

All Rights Reserved

ISBN-13: 978-1-922856-82-1

Copyright ©2024 Larry Ivkovich

V.1.0

Printed in Palatino Linotype.

IFWG Publishing International
Gold Coast

www.ifwgpublishing.com

After a visit to the Railroad Depot Museum in Dennison, Ohio several years ago, I was struck by the town's history during the second World War. From the Museum's website (https://dennisondepot.org/):

> "Recognized as a National Historic Landmark, the Dennison Railroad Depot is the most significant remaining example in the nation of a railroad canteen still reflecting its WWII heritage. During WWII, 1.3 million service members were served free food by 4,000 working volunteers at the Dennison Depot Salvation Army Servicemen's Canteen. These service men and women traveled by troop train along the National Defense Strategic Railway and stopped at the Depot as they were going off to fight in the war."

Parts of the museum were actual train cars containing exhibits you walked through, including one of a hospital train car. I was inspired immediately to write a story based on this and, with my love for 'portal stories,' and a touch of steampunk, *Hope's Song* was born.

One

Mahoning County, Northern Ohio
Gaia American Union
June 1865

The horizon exploded in a wall of fire.

Mirrie Fredrickson recoiled in shock, dropping the bed sheets she had just unpinned from her backyard clothesline. Her golden retrievers, Tar and Pitch, hackles raised, ran in circles, barking and pawing frantically at the grass. A sudden prickling danced across Mirrie's arms and over her scalp. She stared agape, her hands clasped at her chest.

What in heaven? she thought.

An enormous, churning blue cloud roared aflame across the rugged Ohio landscape toward her family's farmstead. A sound, like that of the breaching leviathans Mirrie had seen off the eastern coast, split the cool morning air.

My god. She ran toward the cornfield where her husband and son were harvesting. *This is no earthly storm.* "John!" she cried. "Arden!"

A gust of hot wind slammed into her, knocking her backwards. A noxious smell, a reeking stench of something unnatural, assaulted her senses. Instantly, her jeans and cotton shirt became soaked with a harsh, heavy humidity. Her long, brown hair plastered wetly against her head and neck.

Coughing and gagging, Mirrie pressed forward. She screamed John and Arden's names. They weren't far out in the field. Surely, they could make it back.

A thunderclap jerked her gaze skyward. The blue cloud loomed overhead, blocking out the sun. Pulsing, ghostly halos lit up its swollen mass from within.

The cornfield burst into flame.

"Ugh!" Mirrie fell to her knees, fighting against the heat and wind buffeting her. Her skin crawled as if blanketed by a swarm of insects. The grass beneath her flickered, sparking and smoking. "God, God, no!" she cried. "Arden! John!" The cornfield had become an inferno, a pyre of blue, devouring flame.

She pushed herself to her feet and rushed forward, only to be forced back by the intense heat. She screamed again and again, finally realizing nothing could survive such a conflagration.

Nothing.

"If something ever happens to me," John had told her many times. *"You have to go on without me. You must carry on for your and Arden's sake. Promise me you'll do that."*

But not without both of you! With a gasping sob, Mirrie forced herself to turn and run. Tar and Pitch paced outside the small barn behind the Fredrickson house. Silent now, their eyes widened with terror.

Despite the confusion and fear raging within her, Mirrie acted on impulse. The chickens and cats ranged free and had probably scattered. But she couldn't leave the horses undefended against the encroaching fire.

She rushed into the barn and unlatched the three stalls where the animals stabled. "Run!" she yelled, slapping the horses' rumps and waving her hands. The frightened equines galloped out of the barn's open doors, heading toward the distant low hills of Mahoning County.

"Come on, my boys!" Mirrie cried to Pitch and Tar, approaching panic urging her on. The dogs ran with her behind the barn where the old oak loomed like a towering sentinel. The lofty tree had stood for over a hundred years, ever since the Fredrickson family had settled here. Beneath its wide, leafy canopy, Mirrie yanked open the driver's door to the family's parked ground-mobile. Whining, the retrievers jumped into the back of the steam-powered, four-wheeled vehicle while Mirrie sat behind the steering wheel and shakily activated the motor's flash-boiler.

She turned to look back over her shoulder. The yard and picket fence were ablaze. The house, with its Victorian-style three stories, wraparound porch, and twin gables, were engulfed in flame. Everything she and John had worked for, built... Gone in a single horrendous moment.

A moment beyond comprehension.

They can't be dead, she thought. *They can't be. Please, God...*

At that moment, the blue cloud stopped its destructive advance. It dissipated, burning off like some demon fog. Tendrils of sparkling mist dropped wriggling to the ground. Figures emerged from the blighted, smoking cornfield. For one brief joyous moment, Mirrie thought her prayer had been answered, that John and Arden had survived.

But no. The...*beings* striding toward the burning house weren't her husband and son. John and nine-year-old Arden, whom Mirrie called her Baby Boy, were gone forever. She knew that now. Instead, standing at least seven feet tall with green, reptile skin, possessed of multiple limbs and glowing yellow eyes, these *things* weren't even remotely human.

More appeared until at least a dozen of the sleeveless-robed entities stood in what was left of the Fredrickson back yard. More sat astride huge spider-like creatures. Others towed huge, wheeled, cannon-like machines. One of the lizard-beings turned its glittering gaze in Mirrie's direction. It pointed a clawed finger at her and gave voice to a nightmarish shriek.

Choking back a scream, Mirrie kicked the ground-mobile into gear and spun out of the farmstead. As Tar and Pitch huddled in the back seat, she drove away, jerking and swerving from beneath the oak onto the gravel entry road.

She screeched out onto Highway Sixty-Two, accelerating more smoothly now toward the Anderson farmstead, five miles away. She didn't know what else to do, where else to go. She had to find out what was happening!

She looked to her right, her breath catching in her throat. There, toward Youngstown, more blue smoke mushroomed in the distance. Ahead of her, another fiery explosion lit up the horizon.

The scream she had stifled finally burst free. Tears ran down her cheeks. She hit the steering wheel with her fists, giving voice to the madness threatening to overcome her. "Why? How?" she cried, surrendering to anger and grief. "Oh, John, Arden…"

She knew then what had happened; the stark realization shot through her like ice water. It had finally come to pass. There had been warnings given by the government Tech-Mages, prophecies foretold by shaman Dream-Walkers, preparations made by the Gaia American Union military. All to no avail.

The Dimensional Veil had been breached. Monsters from beyond the Numinous had come into the world.

Two

The Vision-Realm of Ptesan-Wi

It was a dream like no other.

The Lakota hunter stood atop a high escarpment beneath a star-dappled, moonlit sky. *Paha Sapa* rose above and around him like jagged teeth, the sacred Black Hills stark and foreboding. A shimmering aura emanated from the rugged peaks. Ancient power, mystical and unknowing, resounded from their granite cores.

A sense of loss, of yearning for his homeland, rose within the Hunter.

He blinked in surprise. What was this? A soft, blue light flickered and swirled before him like a swarm of fireflies. It hovered on the edge of the escarpment, flowing, undulating, transforming.

For a moment, the Hunter thought his long-lost *mitawin*, his wife Tashina, had returned to him from the Spirit World. His heart leapt in unbridled joy; he opened his mouth to cry her name.

But no. As the azure radiance dimmed to a soft pulse, he beheld a strange Indigene woman. Young-seeming, yes, but her wide, gray eyes smoldered with great age and wisdom. She...*floated* a few paces from him, her beautiful, brown-skinned face illuminated as if by a powerful inner fire.

The Lakota hunter stared. Did his own eyes betray him? No, the woman, her feet encased in beaded moccasins, hovered a hand's length above the rocky ground. Long, dark hair tumbled about her shoulders as if wind-blown, though no breeze was evident. A white, feathered robe draped her tall, slim body.

"You are wondering why you are here, Mahpiya," she intoned softly, her voice as soothing as Love Flute melodies, her expression enigmatic.

Though once a brave and noble warrior, the Hunter shivered with a sudden uncertainty. He faced a woman of immense power, a power which resonated from her like the heat of the sun. Was she a shaman like Tashina had been? She wore a deep aspect, one of far-seeing import. She held him in thrall with her spectral presence. A sudden realization came to him. Could this be the White Buffalo Calf Woman, herself?

"It is so," the woman said, as if reading his thoughts. "I am Ptesan-Wi."

"Is this the vision-realm then?" he asked, awestruck. "How is that so? I am no shaman, no Dream-Walker."

She smiled. "Yet here we are, Mahpiya, immersed in the Numinous."

Mahpiya, his childhood name. No one had called him that since the Battle of Horned Run, when the Lakota, Arapaho, and Cheyenne had fought together against the Demon hordes.

A sudden anger rose within him at the reviled memory, overcoming his caution and doubt. He lashed out at the woman, unmindful of the consequences, his fists clenched at his sides. "You are a goddess of peace! Why have you permitted such killing and destruction? Why have you allowed the Demons to enter our world and attack us?" *To let Tashina and our unborn child die.*

"I am only a herald and cannot interfere." She paused, eyes closed, a sad expression coming over her perfect features. "I grieve for you and those others who have suffered. The Great Mystery is aptly named, even for those such as myself. In this instance, I only know what can be. What *must* be."

The Hunter fell in on himself. A grief he had locked away burst free and crumbled the inner defenses he had constructed so carefully since Tashina's death. "Why?" he asked again. "Why am I here? What do you want of me?"

"Only to tell you to be strong. You doubt, you fear, as all beings do. But you are different. You must persevere. Everything in its own time."

The Hunter felt as if he were falling. "Your words are strange to me," he said. "I do not understand."

The woman fixed a fierce gaze upon him, her form shimmering ghost-like. "Attend me, Mahpiya, you who now call yourself Sky Wolf, Warrior of the Air. You feel your existence has no meaning, yet, in time, when your eyes and heart have been opened, you will partake of the Sacred Pipe's cleansing smoke and your destiny will become clear. The dangers of the path you now walk are what you must endure to achieve oneness. Distasteful as you may find such a violent path, it is necessary to complete our part in the Great Mystery."

Her form wavered like smoke on the wind. Before the Hunter's eyes, Ptesan-Wi, the White Buffalo Calf Woman, vanished.

"No!" Sky Wolf cried, overcome, confused, anguished. "Come back! Return Tashina and our child to me. I beg you."

Afterward, he awoke, sweating in his bedroll, his heart pounding. *What does it mean?* he thought as tears welled in his eyes. *What does it mean?*

Northern Ohio Fringe Lands
Gaia American Union
August 1872, Post-Collapse

Sky Wolf glided the *Nightbird*, his two-seat ornithopter, to a landing behind a tall thicket of scrub brush. A Tech-Mage creation of wood, metal, wires, springs, levers, and pneumatic and hydraulic gears; the winged craft's braking steam-jets slowed it to a silent halt. Its mooring skids gently touched down on the rocky ground.

Sky Wolf unfastened his safety web. Removing his goggles, he climbed from the craft's pilot-seat to its small side running-board. He reached into the backseat and released the safety webbing that kept his bestial comrade secure.

Torra, Sky Wolf's spirit-brother and fellow hunter, growled and leaped from the seat onto the ornithopter's right bat-like wing. Tail whipping behind him, the white cougar shot an irritated gaze at his human. *I am sorry, my brother,* Sky Wolf thought-sent, employing the silent mind-bonding ability he shared with Torra. *But you should be proud. There are no others of your feline kind who can fly like hawks.*

Torra chuffed, shook his great head, and dropped gracefully to the ground. Though the cougar had never gotten used to the 'thopter's flight, Sky Wolf couldn't help but look in amusement at the feline's discomfit. It wasn't so long ago he felt the same way himself.

From the *Nightbird's* storage compartment located behind the back seat, the Lakota hunter retrieved the insulated cold-packs where he would store his rich client's "trophies." He unsheathed his rifle from its onboard scabbard and slung both it and the packs over his broad shoulders.

Stay here, he instructed Torra, tossing him a large piece of deer jerky. Torra ignored the treat, growling. *I know you wish to accompany me, but we have never been in this part of the Fringe Lands before. Keep watch for any danger. I will return shortly.* Sky Wolf turned and sprinted off in the direction of his prey.

Dressed in tan buckskin breechcloth, leggings, tunic-shirt, and moccasin-boots, Sky Wolf blended in with the brown Fringe Lands' terrain. Tall and well-muscled, his speed and serpentine movements made detection difficult in any case. A single long braid of black hair trailed down to the back of his waist where his longknife rested in its leather sheath.

The gently sloping terrain of some of the Midwest land never appealed to Sky Wolf. But the mid and south-eastern region of the Ohio Fringe Lands, with its ridges, hills, and gorges, was much more suitable. After the world had been sundered by the Demons, Sky Wolf had journeyed east. Here, in the Fringe Lands, he had discovered his hunting and tracking skills could be put to the best use. In this wasteland, he could do the most good for himself and Torra to survive.

After the Battle of Horned Run, he, like many of his people, had dispersed. The combined mysticism of the Lakota, Arapaho, and Cheyenne shamans had defeated the Demon horde at that cataclysmic conflict. Their magic sealed off the Demons' prime gateway through the Veil, stopping the flow of larger weapons and flying craft from their own world. But in the process, many shamans had died, their remaining magic-wielding brothers and sisters sorely weakened. The western Indigene nations had scattered as a result.

Sky Wolf's *mitawin*, a powerful shaman in her own right, had joined the other mystical ones at Horned Run. Though close to birthing their first child, Tashina had added her own power to help close the Demon gateway.

Neither she nor her unborn infant had survived.

He'd been too cowardly to take his own life, as some had. Instead, peyote eased the pain of his loss. In rare moments of clarity Sky Wolf thought of partaking of the Sacred Pipe, that celestial gift which *Ptesan-Wi* had bestowed on the Lakota people after coming to the world so very long ago. Sky Wolf had never done so, yet he still carried such a pipe with him, wrapped in cloth. He felt unworthy, though Ptesan-Wi herself had mentioned the sacred object to him in a dream, where he walked within the White Buffalo Woman's vision-realm.

Ptesan-Wi had also spoken of a destiny he must fulfill. Sky Wolf had become a Demon Hunter, a killer-for-hire, bereft of his people and way-of-life. What destiny could he possibly achieve after falling so far?

A quarter mile from where he had landed, he raced to the top of a low bluff and knelt to study his current prey. In the narrow scrub grass-dotted basin below, a small group of Demon Renegades gathered around one of their artificial glowlights. An opposing wind brought the creatures' familiar but still-strange scent to Sky Wolf's flared nostrils. The three Demons hunkered down for their morning meal, the rising sun's orange rays glinting off their scaly bodies. Their two tentacles, one undulating from each shoulder, animated the Demons' overall manner. Foolishly, no guards had been posted.

Such overconfidence would be their undoing.

Sky Wolf unslung the cold-packs and his rifle. He lay on his stomach, stretched out on the rocky hummock, and looked through his weapon's telescopic sight.

How easy it would be to shoot them from here! Renegade Demons, those displaced from their own kind like human refugees, provided Sky Wolf with the means to make a living. Though Sky Wolf hunted for bounty, he preferred to give his prey a chance and not always take such a coward's way in achieving his goal. He had been a warrior once, where honor and courage prevailed. The expectation of battle, the thrill of combat, still coursed through him.

"*Life Slayer*," the Demons called him. For good or ill, Sky Wolf had garnered a dark reputation among their kind. Still, out of respect, and a sense of honor he had mostly given up, he had once allowed a worthy Demon adversary to go free, much to the dismay of his employer.

Still, better to just get this over with. The same employer had rehired him, much to Sky Wolf's surprise. The rich, successful, white businessman, Peter Stamatis, was very impatient and very powerful in the Outlander's world. "*Just bring me their heads!*" he'd ordered. "*Don't waste any time.*"

Their heads. Rich, white Outlanders and others seeking vengeance all harbored a twisted desire to display Demons like trophies. A perverse manner of the Indigene custom of "counting coup". Sickening, Sky Wolf knew. Savage. But he was paid very well for his services.

He took aim at one of the Demons, its lizard face coming into sharp focus, then moved his sights downward to the creature's chest. Best not to damage the vaunted, grisly prize.

Then the Lakota hunter stopped, cocking his head. A tingling warmth danced over his scalp. Crawling away from the edge of the bluff, he directed his attention behind him into the distance. Torra had become agitated, sending a mental warning to Sky Wolf's mind. This was no errant alarm. Never had Torra interrupted him during his kill. Something was wrong.

Torra, he thought-sent. *What troubles you?*

An agitation, a strong desire for Sky Wolf to return, flooded the Lakota's mind. Quickly and quietly, Sky Wolf gathered his packs, descended the bluff, and sprinted back to his flying craft. There Torra paced in front of the *Nightbird*, hackles raised. Sky Wolf knelt and placed a hand against the cat's neck, staring into his bright eyes. *My brother*, he thought-sent. *What have you sensed so urgently?*

The cougar's green orbs bore into Sky Wolf's dark ones; his mouth skinned back to reveal sharp fangs. Slowly, an image coalesced in Sky Wolf's mind. Though abstract and non-human, the powers of the cougar to detect danger and project that danger's nature were powerful indeed. Still, this mental sending of Torra's was unusual. And confusing.

An Outlander refugee camp, Sky Wolf interpreted, puzzled. *What has that to do with us, my brother?*

Torra growled softly, butting his head against Sky Wolf's shoulder. An insistence Sky Wolf had never felt from the cougar radiated like heat from the sun.

Such resolve could not be ignored. Many times, his spirit-brother's mighty senses had helped them, had saved them in battles they had fought together against the Demons. *Very well*, he thought-sent, knowing he could find his current prey again. *Show me.*

Again uncharacteristically, Torra leaped up into the ornithopter's back seat with no urging. Sky Wolf fastened the cougar's webbing, stored the cold-packs, and sheathed his rifle before climbing into the pilot-seat.

He strapped in and donned his goggles. Pushing back a rising uneasiness, he started the craft's small but powerful ignitor and grasped the control-lever. The lifting steam-jets activated, pushing the craft vertically off the ground enough for Sky Wolf to initiate the pneumatic wing-cranks. The *Nightbird's* bat-like pinions lifted it swiftly into the sky.

Three

Northern Ohio Fringe Lands
Fort Ottawa Refugee Camp
August 1872, Post-Collapse

"The Dimensional Veil always protected the Gaia American Union. It cordoned off our world from the other branches of the Numinous, that vast multi-dimensional realm the Tech-Mages refer to as the 'Multiverse'. Then the Kuronts came, who the Indigenes call Demons, who we Outlanders have dubbed Eelees. They blasted through the Veil with their blue-fire, opening gateways into and ravaging our world, changing everything."

Jom sat alone at the inner perimeter of the northern Fringe Lands refugee camp, as he had every evening for the last two months. The remains of Fort Ottawa, an abandoned Indigene stockade, was surrounded on three sides by a tall, palisaded wall. Part of the rear section, its wood damaged and rotting, had been taken down as camp members had erected scaffolding and worked to repair it. A temporary fence had been constructed between the damaged wall section and the jagged gorge which stretched to within a few yards of the stockade.

Jom leaned against the bole of a stunted chestnut tree, relishing a cool late summer breeze. The stars faded slowly in the approaching dawn. The smell of wood smoke drifted pleasantly.

Several yards from Jom's one-eyed vantage point, light from the communal fire-pit and four flickering oil-globes revealed camp members gathered for the after-breakfast meeting. Chetan Atal, the camp leader and former Tech-Mage, stood in the middle of the seated, circled group, his dark brown skin shining in the firelight. His rich, educated voice resounded, retelling the story of the Kuront invasion, the "Day of the Collapse" as it had come to be known.

"There had been predictions, studies, warnings, that such an event could happen. Some preparations had been made but not enough to stop the Veil from collapsing."

Chetan knows a lot, Jom thought. *But kin I tell him what happened to me?* He'd tried to talk to others over the years, tried to tell them his story. No one listened for long, accusing him of being a traitor, a liar, even a Kuront Shifter. He'd been beaten, driven out of other camps. He didn't want to experience that pain again.

Jom absently scratched the left side of his face, caressing the small nub of his left ear. His wounds still itched sometimes from the burning though they'd long ago turned to scar tissue. With the two remaining fingers of his left hand, he absently touched the patch that covered his scabbed-over left eye socket. He had adapted to his injuries over time, managing just as well with only part of his senses.

Jom had the Kuront *scientists,* who had nursed him back to health after the fire, to thank for that. If for nothing else. Jom had, after all, been a prisoner of the Kuronts and subject to their "tests" and "interrogations." The triangular symbol his captors had tattooed on Jom's neck, the mark Jom tried to hide, always set him apart. As such, he couldn't be completely trusted, could he?

Not to mention his appearance, which the Kuronts couldn't completely heal of its burns, the scar tissue too ingrained. "You look bad enough to scare the Eelees back to their world," Carmen, the camp cobbler, had once mocked him, her gray eyes full of distrust. "Our children don't need to see that, Eelee-boy."

Eelee-boy. That wasn't the worst thing Jom had been called but it still cut through him. Sometimes he wondered who had been the cruelest—Kuronts or humans?

The eyepatch he'd devised covered some of his facial damage and, at least, his pullover shirt had a hood sewn onto it, which could further hide his disfigurement. He reached back now and tugged the hood over the tufts of short hair that dotted his head. It was a self-conscious act he performed, done out of habit, even though no one looked his way.

No, that wasn't quite true. As always, the little blonde-haired orphan girl, Hope, stared in his direction from her perch around the fire. She had always seemed to be interested in him but too shy to approach. He wouldn't encourage such contact, of course, for fear of reprisal from the adults.

Still, he couldn't complain of his treatment at Fort Ottawa. Chetan and some of the other members of the camp were kinder and more tolerant than those of the other groups Jom tried to join. Here, at least, he could bed down on their periphery with a borrowed bedroll and share their food. It was better than being completely alone.

In return, he helped to track any wandering game that might be used for food, to harvest the rugged roots and herbs that had begun to grow back in the wastes. A knack for finding underground water was a talent he excelled at. He had survived for two years in the Fringe Lands on his own and had developed some skills.

Behind Jom, one of the camp patrols stood guard on the rampart catwalk above the front gate, rifle in hand. The guards were ever-vigilant for any danger, and alert for other survivors trying to find their way through the Fringe Lands.

But Jom suspected another of their duties was to keep an eye on *him*. Just in case.

"The Kuronts invaded us," Chetan continued, "bringing their death and science with them through multiple gateways they had opened between our world and theirs. The largest of those gateways was sealed off at the Battle of Horned Run. Many of the Lakota, Arapaho, and Cheyenne shamans gave their lives to accomplish that magical task. But other, smaller gateways still exist in Ohio and West Virginia, allowing other Kuronts to come through with weapons and supplies, though their numbers have decreased in the last three years, thankfully, though we're not sure why."

I know, Jom thought. *But they'll never stop comin'.*

The adults gathered around the fire frowned and muttered angrily, their memories still too fresh, too raw. Some of the young ones rarely tired of hearing the tale, the youngest probably never having seen a Kuront. "They attacked without mercy or reason, riding their spider-like Spindlers, destroying everything in their path."

Jom looked away. So much hatred, fear, and distrust existed on both sides. Even for those, like himself and other refugees, who lived between those two worlds.

"Though we were completely surprised by the Kuront attacks, the Gaia Defense Coalition, the indigenous shamans, and the Tech-Mages, reacted swiftly, working together to fight back enough to keep us from being completely overwhelmed. Now, with their prime gateway closed, the odds have been evened somewhat, especially with the Union's development of the Light Cannon. Still, the war continues."

"But we will win, won't we?" Hope asked, her round, blue-eyed face beaming. "Won't we, Chetan?"

Jom sat upright, his senses tingling. The wind had shifted, bringing with it an intense, fruity scent. A hissing Jom knew all too well reached his ear. He jumped to his feet. "Dalawgs!" he shouted, running toward the campfire. "Spindlers!"

As Chetan and the others turned toward him, the alarm tolled, the repurposed school bell ringing. The camp dogs began barking furiously. The sounds of wood splintering, shattering followed. Shots rang out, shouts, curses and screams of terror. Unworldly shrieks rent the night air.

Beyond the fire-pit, large, humped shapes moved among the tents, huts, and outbuildings of the camp. Crab-like appendages flailed, crashing through wood and metal. *No, no, no,* Jom thought, rushing forward. How had feral dalawgs gotten so close, despite the guards and the fence?

A camp member ran past Jom, brandishing a rifle. Chetan barked commands as the communal gathering dispersed. "Lemme help!" Jom cried as he reached the camp leader's side. "I kin help! I know Spindlers!"

Before Chetan could respond, a dalawg scuttled through the smoke of the campfire. Mandibles clacking and drooling, the horse-sized spider-beast loomed over a fallen child. "It's Hope!" Chetan shouted. The young orphan lay on the ground, cowering before the creature.

Without a second thought, Jom sprinted toward the monster.

Four

Hospital train Aesculapius
Northern Toledo/Dennison Railway line
August 1872, Post-Collapse

Nurse Matron Miriam Kosanavic entered the Infirmary Car of the *Aesculapius*. The smells of disinfectant, ether, urine, and blood lingered in the car's close confines, causing Miriam, for just a moment, to falter and lose her balance.

The occasional jerking and vibration of the huge steam-powered conveyances no longer bothered her as they once had. Since Miriam had resumed her nursing career six years ago for the Midwestern branch of the Gaia Defense Coalition, she had served five of those years as Patient Liaison and Nurse Matron for the military railway lines. Riding the great iron troop transports had become second-nature to her. It reminded her of what the sailors of the Leviathan-Class metal-clads involved in the Lake Erie conflicts had once told her about getting their "sea legs".

Yet, the interior of the Infirmary Car, with its wounded and dying, always seemed to upset her equilibrium. *Buck up, Mirrie,* she thought, steadying herself. *Now's not the time to go soft.*

The eight bunk beds, four on each side of the Infirmary Car, were occupied by those seriously wounded in battles with the Eelee invaders. Two men and one woman, members of the GDC's Midwest Regiment lay in various stages of injury and treatment.

All were asleep or medicated at this early morning hour. Corporal Emilio Vega, his eyes bandaged due to a blinding Eelee attack, lay on his side. He faced the window which revealed the ravaged northern Ohio countryside.

She followed his unseeing gaze. Even though the GDC had driven the Eelees back from the Ohio-West Virginia border, the blighted, bare ground showed no signs of recovery, no vegetation poking through the soil. Even nature's resiliency couldn't completely survive the Eelees' destructive blue-fire entries through the Dimensional Veil.

Above the lightening horizon, a military airship hovered into view, its huge cigar-shaped silhouette stark against the cloud-dotted, azure sky. *Heading out to the eastern War Zone,* Miriam reasoned. *Transporting more of the new Light Cannons to fight the Eelees, no doubt. Pray, God, they can do some good!*

Miriam's assistant, Nurse Audra Kingbird, greeted her as the young Ojibwa Indigene finished her work shift. At that moment, a bump in the rails caused the Infirmary Car to really wobble. Both nurses automatically turned and reached out to secure the swinging IV drip-bags beside two of the patients.

Oftentimes, windblown debris got entangled in the rails. Sometimes an animal wandered onto the tracks, the train's massive iron wheels crushing the poor creature. Once or twice, hopeless, disenfranchised refugees had thrown themselves in front of the transport, ending their poor, desperate lives.

"How are they doing?" Miriam asked of the patients when the train's motion smoothed out again.

Audra pursed her lips. Miriam noted her youth, far too young to have experienced the misery the war with the Eelees had caused, but a strong, capable caregiver nevertheless. Audra had spent part of her childhood in a refugee camp, her Indigene stronghold overrun by Eelee invaders. But, unlike many of those displaced unfortunates, she had managed to leave the refugee life behind.

Like Miriam, she wore the long red dress, full-sleeved, white-cuffed shirt, white apron and red nursing short-cap of their GDC Nursing Order. A stylized blue cross was sewn onto the upper right sleeves of their shirts and on the front of their caps. Unlike Miriam's shorter, fuller figure, Audra's tall, slim frame filled out her uniform in a way that made her a favorite among the male soldiers and patients.

"None of their conditions have changed," Audra replied tiredly, a wisp of dark hair peeking out from under her cap. "Mercifully, all are sleeping now though Corporal Vega and I did talk a little." Audra smiled, her tawny features lighting up. "He is a gabber and a flirt, that one."

"So that's what you think of me, eh, Nurse Audra?" Corporal Vega yawned, stretching his lanky form beneath the blanket. "I'm cut to the quick."

"Ah, Corporal," Miriam said gently. "I hope we didn't wake you. How are you doing today?"

"Mornin', Matron," Vega said hoarsely. Through the bandages covering his eyes, his handsome features crinkled up into a wide smile.

"I'm feelin' better today, I think, even though my pride has been sorely wounded by Nurse Audra's remarks."

Audra smiled and squeezed Vega's arm. "I think you'll survive, Corporal."

"That I will, Nurse, especially with your expert care. When'll we get to Dennison?"

"In about two or three hours," Miriam replied. "I take it you've been through there before?" Dennison, Ohio, was a military train hub, a way-station, an oasis for those shipping out to and returning from the various battle fronts. There, the Sisters of the local Rectory of St. Mortimer maintained a canteen, clinic, and recreation hall for the soldiers. The town had become, for many, a second home, a place to prepare for and recuperate from the horrors of war.

"Yes, ma'am," Vega replied. "When I first got conscripted and assigned to the Toledo airship yards. I hope they can raise the Sarge's spirits now like they raised mine then."

Miriam frowned. Sergeant Hannah Parker, the patient lying across the aisle. Bandages also covered her head, the poor woman lying in a coma from her own more serious injuries. "I'm sure they will," she said, a slight hesitation in her voice. "The sisters are miracle workers in that regard."

Vega nodded, evidently not noticing the doubt underlying Miriam's words. Vega and Parker had served together, and he held out hope for his sergeant. The corporal sighed and lay back, once again falling asleep. Miriam noticed the tip of the wooden thumper-club peeking out beneath his blanket. Vega had kept his three-foot long military weapon throughout his ordeal, refusing to part with it.

"Do you want me to take that club away now, Matron?" Audra asked quietly.

Miriam sighed. "No, I don't think so. If it makes him feel more secure, it shouldn't be a problem." *He has been blinded, after all.*

Miriam and Audra rechecked Parker's IV drip-bag then examined the other most seriously wounded patient besides Sergeant Parker, Lieutenant Hokatara, whose left leg had to be amputated above the knee. Both soldiers' prognoses remained dire, despite the medical staff's best efforts.

"Very good then, Audra," Miriam said. "Now you go get your own rest. I'll take over."

"Thank you, Matron."

At that moment, the inter-car speaker-tube whistled from its wall sconce near the emergency surgery cubicle. Miriam gestured for Audra to remain a moment longer. She left the patients' bunk area, picked up the cone-shaped horn, and spoke into its flared end. "Yes? Matron Kosanavic here."

"Matron," the deep voice of Dr. Onta Songetay, the *Aesculapius'* physician, intoned from the other end. "Please join me in the Supply Carriage if you're not otherwise engaged."

"Yes, Doctor." She placed the speaker-tube back into its sconce. "I'm sorry, Audra, can you attend to the patients a little longer? Dr. Songetay needs to talk to me."

"Of course, Matron."

"Thank you." Miriam walked toward the front end of the Infirmary Car, where she pressed the exit plate. The door slid open.

I wonder what Songetay wants to see me about? she wondered as she stepped inside.

Five

Northern Ohio Fringe Lands
Fort Ottawa Refugee Camp

Sky Wolf and Torra approached the edge of a wide, jagged gorge on foot. A shallow chasm in the earth, the gorge snaked to within several yards of the rear of a stockade—the refugee camp Torra had directed him to. The rear wall of the palisaded structure looked to be in repair, some of its timbers taken down, scaffolding erected. The remains of what looked to be a more recently-built fence between the construction and the outside had been broken through.

A bell's tolling, accompanied by gunshots, resounded from the stockade's interior. Explosive bursts of wood splintering, the rending of metal. The screams of those under siege.

Sky Wolf jolted in surprise. Within the stockade yard, two monstrous creatures ran amok. People rushed about in panic before the unnatural attack. More of the interim fence fell beneath two more of the terrifying beasts as they clambered out of the gorge. They crashed through the fort's broken rear opening to join their brutish comrades.

A herd of feral spider-mounts, those monstrous beasts the Demons rode.

Torra shrieked defiantly, his muscles coiled to strike beneath Sky Wolf's hand. Moments earlier, through his monocular, Sky Wolf had observed the stockade from where he landed the *Nightbird*. Yet, though he saw nothing untoward, Torra insisted on getting closer to the fort, growling and pacing and shooting Sky Wolf a look as sharp as the Lakota's longknife. Now, the cougar's hackles raised, his manner bent on attack. *Torra*, Sky Wolf thought-sent, *why have you brought us here? This is none of our concern.*

Indeed, helping these refugees would bring no reward, no coup, and only put him and his spirit-brother in danger. There was no reason…

Torra screamed, whirling to his right. A fifth spider-mount scrabbled up the side of the gorge. Possessed of multiple legs and eyes, the creature resembled a foul, twisted abomination of the trickster-spirit *Iktomi*. It rose and lashed out at Sky Wolf with a double-jointed, sharply-serrated leg.

Caught off-guard, Sky Wolf stumbled backwards. The creature's bladed appendage struck the Lakota's rifle, ripping it from his hand. As Torra pranced sideways to avoid the spider-mount, Sky Wolf fell tumbling to the ground.

He rolled as he hit and regained his feet, unsheathing his longknife in one smooth motion. He stared at the beast, its body larger than a horse and covered with spiky fur and bony plates. Clacking its slavering mandibles, the spider-mount hesitated, as if also appraising its foes.

Screaming a challenge, Torra moved toward the monster. *No, Torra*, Sky Wolf ordered. Doubt, an unfamiliar emotion, took hold of him. He and Torra had never faced a spider-mount before. Though the cougar was more than capable of defending himself, Sky Wolf would not allow him to be put in such unnatural danger. *Leave here. Go!*

Hissing and spitting like a score of serpents, the spider-mount charged.

Despite its seeming ungainliness, the beast moved quickly. Sky Wolf acted on instinct. The Lakota darted away from the brute's scurrying rush, looking for an opening. The monster pivoted and swung another leg at Sky Wolf in a deadly, cutting arc. Sky Wolf ducked, the sharp-edged limb hissing through the air just above his head. He lunged and moved among the beast's legs, dodging and weaving. Grasping the spiky fur on the creature's flank, he hauled himself up onto its back.

Straddling the small hump behind the creature's head as he had seen Demon riders do, Sky Wolf grasped the bony ridge at the base of its skull. Having ignored his human's command to flee, Torra leaped in front of the beast. He slashed at its many eyes, moving sinuously away from the creature's snapping mandibles, only to rush forward again.

The spider-mount bucked like a wild stallion, attempting to shake off its clinging human adversary. At the same time, it tried to back away from its feline one. Sky Wolf raised his longknife and plunged it downward into the creature's noxious flesh.

The spider-mount shrieked, a piercing, unearthly sound. It rolled over on its back to crush its attacker beneath it. Sky Wolf leaped clear, tumbling and rising in a crouch. The brute convulsed, its legs flailing above it. A white blood-like fluid streamed from beneath its head. Sky Wolf had struck a vital spot! A sudden elation rushed through him.

Praise *Wakan-Tanka*, the Great Mystery! He had slain the beast!

Torra trotted up to him, snarling. It was evident in the cat's manner that he didn't consider Sky Wolf's job done. *Very well, my disobedient brother*, Sky Wolf thought-sent. *Since I could not have killed the monster without your help, I will do as you wish.* He wiped his longknife on a patch of scrub grass and sheathed the weapon. He picked up his rifle. *I will see what I can do for the refugees. But only if you move away to a safe place.*

As Torra reluctantly raced off, Sky Wolf skirted the end of the chasm and headed through the breach in the fence for the rear of the stockade. No more spider-mounts exited the gorge. Two mangled human bodies lay among the rubble. He rushed inside to a scene of chaos, staring in shock.

The four remaining feral beasts continued their attack, smashing an outbuilding, striking out at two brave dogs who harried the monsters. A guard on one of the rampart catwalks fired his rifle at the rushing spider-mounts, hitting one then another but only slowing them down.

Part of the rear wall scaffolding still stood. Slinging his rifle over his shoulder, Sky Wolf took hold of a ladder and climbed upward. He reached the catwalk which stretched along the inside of the upper palisade.

Unslinging his weapon, he aimed it at one of the spider-mounts. That's when he saw a girl-child fall before the hideous creature.

A child… The memory of his own unborn swept back to him.

Sky Wolf concentrated his aim at the attacking monster's head. He would not let another child die! But the quick, jerky movements of the spider-mount's jointed legs shielded its head, preventing Sky Wolf from taking a lethal shot.

Then something unexpected happened below, an action Sky Wolf had never seen before. At least one performed by a human.

Tom acted as if controlled by another, just like he had done when he escaped the Kuront compound. His mind reached back to his imprisonment, his Second Life. The Kuronts controlled the dalawgs with thoughts and gestures. The bonding between rider and mount was so intimate that when one of the Kuront riders was killed, its Spindler, as humans called them, would die as well.

But, for whatever reason, a select few of the spider-mounts didn't die when their masters did. These dalawgs became crazed, rogue, forming into wild herds.

Now one of those herds overran the refugee camp.

Jom screamed at the dalawg, waving his arms to distract the beast away from Hope. The creature stopped and directed its gleaming multiple eyes on Jom.

"At's right, at's right!" Jom cried, pushing back the fear building inside him. "You doan wanna hurt her." The Kuronts had let Jom interact with dalawgs, had even allowed him to ride them, after a time. Jom concentrated, focusing his attention on the repulsive creature. He formed a hand-signal used to herd the spider-mounts.

The dalawg backed up a step, cocking its head, perhaps confused by this very un-Kuront-looking being giving him a once-familiar command. "Yuh, yuh, good beastie." Jom slowly inched forward, kneeling and grasping a sobbing Hope under her arms. He pulled the small girl to her feet. Just for a moment, he took his eye off the dalawg.

Too late, Jom realized, as he jerked his attention back to the creature. The spider-mount rubbed a spiky leg against its face. It opened its dark maw, hissed and lunged forward. Jom wrapped Hope in his arms and pushed her to the ground, covering her with his body.

A shot rang out. Jom jerked and looked up. The dalawg's head ruptured into a splattering of skin, bone, and bloody white fluids. It fell sprawling to the ground. Another movement to his left... A figure on the battlement, holding a smoking rifle, a long braid swinging from its head. No one Jom recognized.

Jom blinked and the figure was gone.

Chetan appeared at Jom's side and helped him to his feet. Jom let him gently take Hope from his trembling hands. "Are you all right, girl?" Chetan asked, his dusky features etched with concern. "Jom?"

"I... I..." What had he been thinking? He could have been killed! He was no hero! "I'm all right."

Carmen raced into the firelight, rifle in hand. "We killed two of 'em, Chetan," the cobbler said. "Head shots did it. Wounded another but it ran off."

"Good shot, Carmen," Chetan said, indicating the dead dalawg.

"Wasn't me," Carmen replied, frowning at the dalawg corpse. "Don't know who got this one. Plus, there's a dead one out by the gorge. Looks like it might of been stabbed."

"Stabbed?" Chetan frowned. "Who among us would be that brave or foolish?"

"Rosa says she saw someone enterin' the back of the fort as the Spindlers attacked. Said he looked like an Indigene and swears he had a white cougar with him."

"A white cougar?" Chetan said. "How strange."

"And I saw someone on the catwalk, shootin'," Jom said. "He weren't from the camp."

"It seems we had a mysterious protector." Chetan frowned, a thoughtful look creasing his features. "We'll talk about that later. Were there any casualties?"

The cobbler's eyes flashed in the firelight. "James and Sharon, who were guardin' the repair site. James was killed and Sharon hurt pretty bad. Doc's seein' to her now. But that's how the fuckin' Spindlers got in. It looks like the monsters snuck up through the gorge. Filthy, connivin' things!"

"Damn it." Chetan let out an exasperated breath. "What about in camp?"

"A few injured though not bad. Most of the back fence is down and there's damage to some of the outbuildings but we were really lucky, considerin'." Carmen turned her attention to Jom, a scowl transforming her weathered face. "You controllin' the Spindlers, Eelee-boy?" she rasped, raising her weapon. "You makin' them attack us?"

"Carmen!" Chetan said. "That's not what happened! He warned us and tried to save Hope. Put your gun down."

Hope wriggled free of Chetan's grasp and ran to Jom. Rising only to his chest, she wrapped her arms around him and squeezed hard. "Thank you, Jom," she said, burying her tearful face against his shirt. "Thank you."

Jom's breath caught in his throat. No one had hugged him in such a very, very long time. Slowly, he returned the orphan's embrace. He closed his eye and, far away, as if in a dream, he heard Carmen and Chetan arguing.

The boy communed with the spider-mount.
Standing with Torra at the base of a small ridge where he'd concealed the *Nightbird*, Sky Wolf recalled the scene he witnessed at the stockade. The spider-mount loomed over the girl-child when a camp-dweller, a boy, rushed in front of the creature. The boy had used the same signing motions Sky Wolf had seen Demons use to direct their own spider-mounts.

Though not entirely successful, the boy's actions had distracted the monster enough for Sky Wolf to shoot and kill the beast. The boy had also shielded the girl with his own body. Courage, indeed.

I would know more about this boy, Sky Wolf thought. The boy had been willing to sacrifice his own life to save the girl. How long had it been since Sky Wolf had acted so selflessly? He rubbed Torra's head and back. *Perhaps this is what you have brought me here for eh, my brother? To shame me?*

Torra blinked, purring.

Once more Sky Wolf recalled the dream-teachings of *Ptesan-Wi*, her mention of following his path. *Destiny*, he mused. He bent down to face Torra. *We have a new hunt*, he though-sent. *We will keep watch on the stockade and the boy who resides within. You sense he is different, do you not? That he is important in some manner?*

Torra blinked again, rumbling deep within his throat. Sky Wolf looked inward, remembering. He and Torra had been together for almost five years.

He'd found the injured and starving young cougar during his travels after Horned Run. Sky Wolf was drawn to the animal, not only because of the cougar's injuries, but also because of the unusual color of his fur. Sky Wolf's thoughts had reached out as if of their own accord. They intertwined with Torra's, forming a powerful bond between human and beast. He treated the cougar with herbs, buffalo hair, and crystals from his medicine pouch, and fed the animal. As a result, Sky Wolf and Torra became spirit-brothers. They grew stronger together and, shortly thereafter, Sky Wolf secured his first paying hunt.

And so, my persistent friend, Sky Wolf though-sent with a resigned sigh escaping his lips. *We will see where this new path takes us.*

Once again, his employer would not be happy.

Six

**Private Locomotive Lionheart
Northern Ohio Fringe Lands
Toledo Railway Branch Line**

"Damn that Lakota freak!"

Peter Stamatis paced the carpeted length of his luxury parlor-coach, his dark-complexioned, mustached features turned downward in an angry scowl. Ignoring the humming gears of his prosthetic right leg, he turned to one of the coach windows and pulled the drapes aside.

The stark landscape of the Ohio Fringe Lands sprawled out and away from his private steam locomotive and its four-car carriage-line. Per his routine operations, this location on the rarely-used branch line served as a rendezvous point for the Renegade hunts. "Sky Wolf was supposed to be here hours ago," he said, running a hand through his long, gray-streaked, black hair. "If he's allowed an Eelee to go free again, I'll have him and that filthy animal of his shot out of the sky!"

"He has never been late before, sir," his aide Willem commented softly. Stamatis brought his attention back to where the elderly German stood by the parlor-coach's mahogany sideboard. Dressed in a black waistcoat over a white shirt, and wearing black pants and shoes, Willem looked every inch the loyal servant. Which he was, but Stamatis knew that never stopped his aide from arguing with or contradicting him at times. "Even when he aborted that hunt," Willem continued, a slight accent underlying his words. "Which, if you remember, he did refuse payment for."

"I wouldn't have paid him anyway," Stamatis replied. "As you well know."

Undaunted, Willem continued, "Still, if nothing else, sir, Sky Wolf is honest and reliable and Torra is quite a clean beast, having petted him myself. Perhaps something unforeseen has happened to them. It's likely your agents stationed in the Fringe Lands may know and report in."

That damn cougar hated Stamatis, always growling and spitting at him! Stamatis glared at Willem. His aide's stoic and reasonable nature was on full display, making Willem one of the few people besides his wife Stamatis couldn't intimidate. Serving in the German military during the Northland Barbarian Uprising had certainly given the man a spine. Well, that characteristic *was* one of the reasons Stamatis had recruited him. "Good thing you're so competent," he said dryly. "Else you'd be looking for a new position."

Willem bowed his white-haired head, knowing full well his value to his superior. "I understand, sir. I am indeed fortunate to be in your employ."

"Don't push it, Willem," Stamatis said, grinning wickedly. "I can send you back to your little Rhineland village in a heartbeat."

"Oh, my god, you two. Stop it. Willem's right, Peter. Something may have delayed the Indigene." Stamatis' wife, Alberta, sat in one of the parlor's plush settees, holding a near-empty glass of bourbon. She, like many of her high-society friends, wore the latest casual attire. A long-sleeve blousy shirt and vest, trousers, and knee boots. Short, bobbed, black hair crowned a thin, sharp-featured face. Matching opal necklace, earrings, and rings rounded out her ensemble. Even during wartime, those with money could afford or commission the newest, most expensive styles.

Fifteen years younger than her husband, Alberta didn't always share her husband's business interests. That had never been a consideration in her marriage to Stamatis, as he well knew. The Eelee hunts, however, were another matter. Sometimes, Stamatis thought, she was more obsessed with their "trophies" than he was.

Plus, she too liked to goad him, especially when she'd had too much to drink. It was a concession in their relationship he mostly overlooked. Mostly. "I was thinking, love," she purred, rising gracefully to her feet despite the liquor she'd consumed. "Maybe we should be helping those poor Renegade Eelees instead of killing them and mounting their heads on the wall."

"Well...*love*," Stamatis allowed himself to fall into their familiar, if irritating, banter. "Those 'trophies' are being studied by my Tech-Mages for any weaknesses, anything we can use against these monsters."

"Oh?" Alberta glanced upward through her long lashes, her brown eyes flashing. "And you don't get just a little bit of pleasure out of seeing them killed?"

"As you do?" He smiled, his own gaze piercing. "How many humans have the Eelees slaughtered and maimed?" He slapped a palm against his thigh above its wood and metal prosthesis. "I can't serve in the GDC to fight against them, but, besides the weapons my factories supply, these hunts are one way I can help rid the world of those alien scum."

"Ah, and there it is. Your leg again..."

"So, you approve of what happened to my leg?" Stamatis' hackles raised just a little. Despite her penchant for cruelty, Alberta rarely brought up that delicate subject.

Alberta snorted. "Oh, don't be ridiculous. I hate what the Eelees have done, and you know it. Especially to us. They should all be slaughtered. But business has been good, hasn't it?" No argument there. Stamatis Armaments, Inc. had certainly turned a profit. Particularly since the war started. "It just feels like you're using these hunts as an excuse for revenge because of your leg."

"As you're using your own injury?" There, he'd said it. He could be as pointed as she could when he wanted.

Alberta's expression hardened. Her free hand rose to her breasts then dropped to her side. "Perhaps. But the Tech-Mages are no closer to figuring out the Eelees now than when the war started. And how many of their heads or brains or whatever they study do they need? Not that I care, mind you." She flashed a twisted smile of her own.

Before he could reply, Alberta brushed by him. "Madame," Willem said with a nod as she exited the parlor-coach to Stamatis' Office Car. No doubt she headed for the sleeper-car where she kept her private bourbon stash.

Stamatis watched her leave then once again moved to the window. "I'll be in my office, Willem," he announced finally. "And fetch me a whiskey, will you? I can use a drink too."

"Sir, if I may?" To Willem's credit, he paused, looking uncomfortable. "Shouldn't you tell Madame the real reason your Tech-Mages are studying the Eelee heads? She deserves to know."

"Not yet," Stamatis said. He had kept things from Alberta over the years, as he was certain she had harbored secrets of her own. It had been necessary to bring Willem in on this specific project and he had sworn him to secrecy. "I appreciate your concern, but the time isn't right. Not until the Tech-Mages are certain it can be done."

Alberta had contracted cancer, a type slow-growing but untreatable, certain she'd contracted it from the same Eelee blue-fire attack which had taken Stamatis' leg. Stamatis was sure he'd found a way to save her, regardless how she'd become ill. And he could benefit from the same treatment, if the money he paid for the hunts would pan out,

Blood money.

Seven

Fort Ottawa Refugee Camp

Throughout the morning, the injured were tended to and the patrol guards doubled. The three dalawg corpses were dragged outside the stockade and burned. What remained of James' body was recovered, a service to be held for him later.

Plans were discussed to put up a new interim fence at the repair site and possibly fill in the end of the gorge with rock and dirt. That would, at least, give more warning if the Spindlers tried to sneak up on them again.

Jom lent a hand sorting out the damage, helping to clean up and to extinguish a number of small fires caused by the dalawgs' savagery. News of his bravery and selfless act had spread quickly. Though still wary, the camp members allowed him to help.

Now, an exhausted Jom leaned against the stockade wall. All during the cleanup, Hope never left his side, refusing to be put to bed. "I don't think you're ugly," she'd said with a shy smile. "And I think you'd look better without that eyepatch."

"You best be goin'," Jom said to her now, absently touching his covered left eye. "You doan wanna be seen with me too much. Some people woan like that."

"You mean Carmen? Ha! I'm not afraid of her." Hope stood with her hands on her hips, her chin lifted defiantly. Dressed in tattered woolen trousers and cotton shirt, her feet clad in Indigene moccasins, she resembled a miniature version of just about every other refugee Jom had encountered.

Despite himself, Jom smiled at the girl's gutsy reply and determined manner. She certainly didn't seem shy now! And why would she be? She had turned up with her sick mother at the stockade gate the previous year, Jom had been told. The mother had died a few days later while Hope wouldn't or couldn't talk. Whatever horror she had lived through had rendered her mute. Slowly, her voice and her precocious nature had come back. Surviving the Fringe Lands took strength, courage, and resolve, even for one so young. Especially for one so young.

"Anyway, I've nowhere to go," she continued, "and everywhere. Since Mama and Papa died, sometimes I stay with Helen and Marilyn and their kids, sometimes with Chetan and his wife. Sometimes I even stay with Carmen, though she snores when she sleeps. I'm eight years old and can stay wherever I want with whoever I want. And I want to stay with you."

Eight years old, Jom thought. *A year younger'n me when I got took by the Kuronts.*

"What did they do to you?" Hope said, her manner serious. "The Eelees. Did they hurt you?" Jom shook his head. He'd never talked to anyone about those years as a captive. He didn't know where to start.

"Looks like you've made a friend." Chetan walked toward Jom, holding out his hand. He too looked tired, his shirt and trousers stained with dirt and sweat. Marilyn Kovatel accompanied him. She was a thin but strong-willed woman, short, gray-streaked hair crowning an oval face. Likewise, her clothing was soiled from the cleanup.

Jom tentatively shook Chetan's hand, surprised at the action. "You did well, Jom," the camp leader said.

"Marilyn, Chetan, he saved me!" Hope cried, a brilliant smile lighting up her face.

The older woman smiled. "I know sweetie," she said. "He's very brave."

"Tha...thank you." Jom looked down, unsure how to respond to such rare attention. Though both Chetan and Marilyn had been instrumental in getting Jom accepted into the camp, contact with them had still been infrequent. Carmen walked by, shooting Jom a look, her expression unreadable.

"I've been very remiss in getting to know you, Jom. I regret that," Chetan said. "I've never asked you before, but do you know where your home is? Your real home."

Gone. All gone. "Not...not anymore."

Chetan pursed his lips, reflecting on that answer before saying, "Later, Marilyn is escorting a small group to the Toledo/Dennison railway line. The Spindler attack has shaken some of us pretty badly."

Jom nodded. Those refugees who were seriously ill or desiring to return to civilization would periodically attempt to flag down one of the troop or supply transports that regularly crisscrossed Ohio. Sometimes the great iron conveyances picked up those who had fled the places destroyed by the Kuronts, who had tired of the refugee existence, desperate for something better, or at least a remnant of their previous lives. But sometimes the trains just sped on by, leaving disappointment and anguish in their rushing wakes.

"How would you like to go with them?"

Jom blinked, startled. "Me?"

"The way you handled the Spindler. That hand-motion. Your imprisonment with the Kuronts could prove valuable to the military. You could provide knowledge that might help them. Have you ever thought of that?"

"Yuh, I have. But I...I'm afraid." Jom looked down, suddenly ashamed, resentful of admitting his fear. He'd been a farm boy, in what he termed his "First Life". Then, he'd been raised in the Kuront compound, if "raised" was the correct word, kept a virtual prisoner, studied like a caged animal. His "Second Life".

And now, because of that, Chetan and Marilyn offered him a way to possibly find his way back to the world.

Chetan squeezed Jom's shoulder. "I understand your reluctance but there's something else that might convince you. We've received news the Tech-Mages, medical doctors, and shamans are working together to help the wounded and sick, combining their abilities in new ways to treat injuries. You may be able to get help for your scars. No one can do anything for you out here."

Jom inadvertently touched his face again. Help for his scars? He had never thought of that happening. "But you used to be a Tech-Mage," he blurted out. "Can't...can't you help me?"

A sad smile spread over Chetan's face. "No," he said simply. "Not anymore."

"You're welcome to come with us, Jom," Marilyn said. "Though you can stay here if you want. It's your decision. You helped us today and we feel we should help you. In turn, you may be able to aid the war effort, do something important."

"I..." Jom didn't know what to say. He felt as if a huge burden had been placed on his shoulders. Him? Help fight against the Kuronts?

"It's a lot to ask, I know," Marilyn added. "But look how you've survived, how you've not been turned by the Eelees. That speaks of an inner strength most of us don't have."

"You know some of us can't go back," Chetan said, his expression turning inward. "Else one of us would come with you."

Yes, Jom knew. It was like that in the other camps and with solitary refugees he had encountered. It wasn't just the Kuront attacks which had driven so many out into the Fringe Lands. Crimes left unpunished, debts left unpaid, promises left unfulfilled, lives too ruined to return to. Marilyn had once been a teacher. What had she and Chetan done to deserve this self-banishment?

But did Jom really have a chance? If he could be of use, if he could do something to help, shouldn't he at least try? His mother and father had always told him he was strong, smart, that he could accomplish anything he set his mind to.

His mother and father...

Hope interrupted his thoughts, crying out, "Yes! I'm coming too!" She ran off excitedly to intercept a camp guard walking by to tell him of her decision.

"Looks like Hope's decided for the both of you," Marilyn said with a smile. "We think she can be helped too."

"How?" Jom watched Hope happily talking to the guard, spreading her good news.

"Before she died, her mother told us Hope could sing like an angel. Even though she's got her voice back, she hasn't sung a note since she's been with us."

"Not all injuries are physical," Chetan added. "We've done all we can with her, and she's much improved, but sometimes she still cries at night."

Like me. "All right. I'll do it."

Chetan smiled. "Best try to get some rest then and something to eat. Marilyn and her group'll be leaving in a few hours."

"Yuh, will...will do." He frowned at Hope, who had returned and stood smiling up at him. "You're a troublemaker," he said, not unkindly. Hope's grin simply grew wider as she took hold of his hand with both of hers.

As Chetan and Marilyn walked off, Jom remembered the gunman he had seen on the battlements. The one who had saved him and Hope. *I wonder who he was,* he thought.

Eight

Hospital train *Aesculapius*

Miriam paused on the exterior coupling platform between the Infirmary Car and the Supply Carriage. The train's juddering motion always felt rockier outside, causing her to hold tightly to the platform railing. She watched the scorched landscape race by, a now-familiar sight she took for granted. But, once again, a sense of foreboding washed over her. *Why do I feel this way?* she thought, perplexed. She had never been prescient like shaman Dream-Walkers but now a feeling of...anticipation nagged at her.

If only she had felt that same sense before. Miriam had lost her son and husband to the Eelees seven years ago when the reptilian creatures had first burst through the Dimensional Veil. She hadn't been able to help her family then and so, in her frustration and desire to help, had subsequently joined the Gaia Defense Coalition Nursing Order. Her assignments with the GDC allowed her to do something to fight back against the invaders.

Yet now, like earlier when she felt off-kilter in the Infirmary Car, she hesitated, as if waiting for...something.

"Everythin' all right, Matron?"

Miriam jumped at the voice intoning above. She looked up to see a GDC sharpshooter peering down over the edge of the Supply Carriage roof. Smoke from the locomotive's stack streamed above him. The sharpshooters were stationed in the rooftop surveillance-sheds built atop every rail-car except the engine and tender carriages. Part of the *Aesculapius'* defense system, the riflemen were always on the alert for bandits or any other danger to the hospital train.

"Sorry, Ma'am, didn't mean to scare you. Just got out to stretch my legs."

Miriam waved, smiling. How did they keep their balance up there? "That's all right. And I'm fine, thank you." Taking a deep breath, she crossed to the Supply Carriage deck, pushed the car's entry plate, and entered. Stacked crates of armaments, equipment, and medical provisions greeted her eyes, rising on both sides of the carriage. A food storage refrigeration unit, powered by its own steam generator, took up space at the far end. In the middle of the carriage stood Dr. Songetay and Lieutenant Josias Camden, the Gaia Defense Coalition officer in charge of the *Aesculapius'* defense system.

"Thank you, Matron," Songetay said. "Even though the patients are sleeping, I didn't want to take a chance they still might overhear us."

A red headband held back Songetay' long, white-streaked, dark hair. An Ojibwe Indigene, Songetay also served as a shaman, at times combining his medical skills with his native people's mysticism. He bore a small tattoo of his clan's bear totem on one cheek and wore white, wrinkled linen trousers and shirt.

"Yes, Doctor?" Miriam asked.

"Lieutenant Camden has some news," Songetay said, his expression more somber than usual. Another momentary apprehension raced through Miriam. She turned toward Camden.

"Good morning, Lieutenant."

"How do, Matron," Camden replied, touching the front of his beret. Tall, lanky, and middle-aged, the mustached black man always reminded Miriam of a scarecrow in his blue GDC uniform, never quite filling out the perpetually ill-fitting jacket and trousers. His large, booted feet splayed outward in a duck-footed stance. "Can't say this is all good though, God willin', it could be nothin' in the end."

Miriam noticed the sidelong glance Camden flicked at Songetay. She sensed the Lieutenant harbored some doubts. He didn't quite believe his own words. "We just received a telegraph message that a group of Kuronts was intercepted by one of our airships only a couple of miles from here. They had a Blue-Fire Blaster with them."

Kuronts. The name the invaders called themselves. Miriam blinked in surprise. "Eelees? Truly?"

"Yes, Ma'am," Camden continued. "As far as we know, this is the first time since the Ohio-West Virginia border offensive that Kuronts have been sighted in the Fringe Lands this far north. Not sure why they're out here now, but they were all ridin' Spindlers. Our ship, the *G.A.U. DragonEye,* managed to wipe out most of the Kuronts with their newly mounted Light Cannons, damagin' the Blaster in the process."

"Praise God for that."

"True enough, Matron, but just before our troops hit that cursed weapon, the Kuronts managed to wing the DragonEye with a blue-fire bolt, inflictin' some damage. It's limpin' back to the Toledo Airship Yards for repairs."

"Were any of our troops wounded?"

"No, Ma'am. Thankfully. But a handful of the Kuronts got away and were reported headin' in our direction. I just want y'all to be aware of the possibility of an attack on the train, slight though it may be. Y'all know how fast the Spindlers can run! Those damn spider-crabs could overtake us easy enough. Excuse my language, Matron."

"I just saw an airship heading east," Miriam said.

"That was the *DragonEye*, all right. Otherwise we could of contacted them for help." With that, Camden bowed to Miriam, nodded to Songetay, turned, and exited the carriage.

"Well," Miriam said, releasing a held breath. "Never a dull moment, is there?"

A flicker of a smile crossed Songetay' lined face. "No, indeed. I trust you'll let Nurse Kingbird know of this development?"

"Of course." Miriam felt a sudden sense of unreality, like on the Day of the Collapse. She tamped down the sensation and asked, "Do you think there's any danger of us being attacked before we reach Dennison?" In all her years of riding the trains, Miriam had never experienced such an assault.

Songetay shrugged his broad shoulders. "Hard to say. We've always been told the Eelees exhausted most of their blue-fire source when they burst through the Veil, so their Blasters aren't nearly as powerful. Still, they can do some damage. In the meantime, let's just concentrate on our patients and let Camden and his men do their job, shall we? Hokatara and Parker will need constant monitoring until we can deliver them to the Dennison Clinic."

A frown crossed Songetay' rugged features. Miriam knew he felt badly for those two patients, for his inability to help them. Even the Ojibwe curing ceremonies and healing songs he had employed had been unsuccessful in their treatment. Sometimes such shamanistic mysticism was effective, but not always.

The doctor fixed a stern gaze upon Miriam. She took a deep breath, expecting more bad news. But, instead, Songetay surprised her with his next remark. "May I ask you to do me a favor, Miriam?"

Miriam cocked a plucked eyebrow. It wasn't often the doctor asked for assistance outside of a medical nature let alone addressing her in so personal a manner. "Of course, Doctor. Anything."

"One of the women in the Lounge Car suffers from a deep depression, more so than I've seen in a wounded soldier. She's very withdrawn, staying away from the others, not eating or drinking, and barely reacting to the simplest of questions."

"Hmmm. And you'd like me to talk to her?"

"If you would, please. It would be good for her to be more responsive before we reach Dennison, so she'll be able to adjust more readily. As Patient Liaison, you have a talent for drawing a person out of themselves in such cases."

A rare compliment. Another surprise. "Thank you, Doctor. Who is she?"

"Her name is Corson. Private Thelma Corson."

Nine

Fort Ottawa Refugee Camp

"*In time, you will forget your human life…those others you knew. That is not necessarily a bad thing.*" *The Kuront scientist cocked its serpent head, its unblinking yellow eyes wide and staring. The tentacles sprouting from its shoulders rippled; the small crest on its head stood erect. "We thought it would have happened by now, but you have proven most resilient."*

Tom moaned in his sleep, the nightmare—the *memory*—returning. In fits and starts, those images of his Second Life emerged through a gauzy veil.

In that strange, clicking language he had been forced to learn, the Kuront continued, "We came to your world to escape famine and plague in our own."

"You are the plague," he replied in the alien tongue. Bitterness and anger edged his words. He stood up from his study desk, his fists clenched at his side. "You started the war here."

"Yes," the scientist replied. "Out of fear and ignorance. But not all of us want to continue this conflict. Some of us want peace. We cannot return to our own world through the portal because of the plague. We want, need, to coexist here."

"But more and more of your kind not affected by the plague cross over into this world with weapons. When will it end?"

"When those of us who desire peace convince the others."

Tom rolled over onto his back, his head snapping first to the right and then to the left in distress. He muttered in his sleep. The same clicks and whistles of his alien captors' language escaped his lips.

"Jom!" a voice cried from somewhere. "Wake up!"

"I do not believe you," he said defiantly. "There has been no talk of peace on either side. I have heard others mention it so."

"And, yet, I speak truly." The serpent tongue of the Kuront flicked out. "You would do well to no longer resist, though your strength and determination are admirable. It is inevitable you will become subservient to us. Or die. We have learned all we have been able to learn from you in your time with us. Become one of us. Perhaps, through you, we can convince the humans we do want peace. At least, that some of us do."

He shivered. Despite his ill-fitting tunic and trousers, a chill shot through him under the Kuront's piercing, enigmatic, alien gaze. Strange, bewildering, dreamlike. The Kuronts wanted him to help them end the war? How could he believe the words of such a creature after all he'd been through?

"It ain't true," Jom mumbled. "It ain't true. They're monsters! They killed father…"

"Jom, please! You're scaring me."

Multiple ear-splitting wails erupted. The alarms of the Kuront Fringe Lands compound sounded like the banshee cries of dying harpies. The habitat cell he studied and slept in, his prison since he'd been a child, shuddered as if from a great impact. The floor beneath him vibrated.

"No, no," Jom moaned, his hands clawing at the bedroll. "Not agin, not agin."

The imprisoning membrane, which surrounded the habitat cell's interior, sparked and hissed. Crying out, he fell to his knees as the very air around him glimmered like stars. The membrane winked out, leaving him…free.

Free!

The scientist whirled away from him. It passed its clawed hand over the entry key-orb, the door irising open. The Kuront stepped out into the habitat corridor. Rushing forward, he followed. Smoke filled the passageway.

The Kuront turned to stare at him. "Go," it hissed, its unexpected words accompanied by a soft whistling. "Run!"

Without a second thought, he raced down the tubular hallway and headed for the exit. The end of the corridor lay torn and open as if by raked by a giant *claw. He jumped outside through the ragged metal…*

"Have to run, have to git away!"
"Jom! Wake up!"

Above the compound, immense, metal-clad airships belched blazing light from their studded underbellies. Thin, radiant beams struck the compound habitat buildings, their protective domes and force-barriers, many of the flying craft the Kuronts had brought from their world, the Kuronts themselves. Explosions erupted around him, the screams of the wounded and dying. Geysers of smoke and fire vaulted skyward. Fire…

Fire!

"Aaaahhhhh!" Jom lurched awake, holding his hands out in front of him.

"Jom, Jom, are you all right?" Hope knelt at his side, her elfin features creased with worry. "You fell asleep and began talking like the Eelees. And screaming about fire."

He trembled. "I'm… Yuh, it's all right, Hope." But the memory continued, even as he tried to shake it from him. He couldn't stop it.

"What did you dream about, Jom? What did you see?"

He'd fled the compound, crouching behind a group of boulders, his chest heaving, his mind awhirl. He directed his one-eyed gaze back toward the destruction he'd left behind. The three airships, immense, human-made raptors, had ceased their lambent barrage, hovering above what was left of the burning Kuront compound. Long, flexible cables snaked down from the flying craft, human soldiers sliding down their serpentine lengths.

Humans. *He* was human! He had remained human despite what the Kuronts had put him through. Here was his chance to rejoin his people. He could…he could…

He choked back a cry. His face and hand, the wounds, and scarring. The disfigurement inflicted on him as a child was horrible. Even he couldn't stomach the sight of his reflection after all this time. Even a Kuront Healer brought in to tend to him had been unsuccessful in mending him fully, too much time having passed.

Plus, the symbol tattooed on his neck would identify him as a prisoner of the aliens. Or worse. The soldiers might suspect him of being a spy, a collaborator, possibly even a Shifter. They might take him prisoner or kill him outright.

In that sense, he had been a captive of the Kuronts for too long. It was too late for him. Jom turned and fled, not looking back.

Until the loneliness and curiosity became unbearable.

And now, after the Kuront scientist told him he could help end the conflict between Kuronts and humans, Chetan and Marilyn had suggested Jom could help the war effort as well! Why him? Why was he so…so important?

Or was he simply someone in the wrong places at the wrong times? He couldn't be that special. Not him.

"Jom," Hope said, shaking him gently. "It's time. Marilyn and the others are waiting. We have to go."

Ten

Northern Ohio Fringe Lands

Torra loped into view, his jaws full of dead rabbits.

Three, my brother? Sky Wolf chided mentally. *You could only fit three fat rabbits in your mouth?*

Torra dropped the fresh kill at his human's feet, looked up at Sky Wolf, and licked his bloody chops. With a soft chuff, he calmly sat back on his haunches. *Well,* his expression seemed to imply, *what are you waiting for?*

Ah, so I am to cook these for you, eh? Sky Wolf allowed a rare grin to spread over his face. *Never have I known a wild beast to prefer his meat roasted. I have spoiled you, it seems.* He knelt and rubbed his spirit-brother's head, scratching the cougar's chest to be rewarded by Torra's loud purring. How the feline could find such well-fed game in this wasteland had always been a mystery to Sky Wolf. Even when they hunted food together, Torra always flushed out those animals long thought to have vanished from the Fringe Lands.

Another type of magic. Perhaps Torra too was a shaman. It was a thought which had crossed Sky Wolf's mind more than once. The cougar was so different, so unusual, in many ways.

He had already set up his small cooking grate and pulled out a pan and bowls. After skinning and gutting the rabbits, he fried them in deer fat. As they ate, Sky Wolf sat back to wait.

He didn't have to wait very long. Only a few hours after the spider-mount attack, a small group of refugees left the stockade and headed south. All traveled on-foot, carrying a modicum of possessions and supplies. Two armed men acted as escorts and guards.

Sky Wolf watched them through his monocular. The boy and the girl-child were part of the departing company. The child held tightly to the boy's hand, staying close to him. A woman seemed to be the leader of the group, directing the others.

Sky Wolf noted the scars covering the boy's face, the eyepatch he wore. *Burns,* he reasoned. *That one has suffered. Could it have been at the hands of the Demons?*

He waited until the group had traveled a short distance from the stockade. After packing up his gear, he powered up the ornithopter and lifted off. He flew low until out of sight of the stockade, then ascended to a height where he would attract little notice (the 'thopter's engines were very quiet, at any rate, ideal for Sky Wolf's surreptitious outings). From this elevation, even if detected, the *Nightbird* could be mistaken for an eagle in full glide, a hawk on the hunt, a vulture searching for carrion, or even one of the strange bird-creatures called harpies that had come from the Demons' world. Torra remained quiet, not hissing or spitting his usual disapproval of this mode of travel.

Sky Wolf had considered simply confronting the boy. Even now, he could announce his presence by using the ornithopter's control panel ampli-phone. The clever sound magnifier would broadcast his voice through the craft's front-mounted speaker-tube. The Tech-Mage Sky Wolf had purchased the craft from after his third lucrative hunt had added some novel ideas to the craft's design including a *diamonite-*reinforced fuselage and the speaker-tube itself.

But he had decided not to reveal himself yet. It was important to remain as quiet and secretive as possible. He needed to watch, observe, gather more information, though, in truth, he wasn't exactly sure why. *What mystery have you gotten me into, Torra?* he thought-sent.

A snort was the only reply.

At the same time, Sky Wolf knew the rich Outlander who employed him also had agents and informants keeping watch in the Fringe Lands for Eelee activity and any other occurrences which might prove lucrative. One such agent may have been at the Refugee Camp and seen the *Nightbird* taking off. The agent, with whatever shadowy method devised, would report to Peter Stamatis.

No matter. Sky Wolf had made his decision. He kept the refugees in sight. He guessed where they might be headed and what they desired to do. He had seen such sometimes-futile action before.

As if in response to his earlier thoughts, a group of three harpies dropped from the clouds above him. Despite Torra's warning growls, Sky Wolf knew the harpies presented no danger. Bat-like in appearance, and as large as a small child, the strange-looking creatures subsisted on a diet of whatever fruits, nuts, grubs, worms, and the occasional birds, they could find. Two flanked the Nightbird, the third gliding in front of the 'thopter, matching its flight.

Sky Wolf smiled at their playful nature as, after a few moments, the harpies flew off. During his hunts, Sky Wolf had caught glimpses of other strange beasts that had entered through the Demon gateways. Many had adapted and survived.

As he had done.

Eleven

Northern Ohio Fringe Lands
Northern Toledo/Dennison Railway line

The memory of his escape from the Kuronts was a never-healed scar of another kind. Yes, Jom had resisted. He would always resist. And the scientist was wrong. Despite taking the name given him by his captors, despite wearing the clothes made for him, despite the years of imprisonment and isolation, Jom would never forget.

But, he realized with some dismay, he couldn't remember exactly what his mother looked like. It had been so long ago yet the pain of losing her still lingered.

His father had truly died. He had saved Jom by throwing himself on top of his son as the blue-fire raged over and around them. But, sometimes, he wondered if his mother had managed to survive. Thankfully, the memory of her sweet voice had remained. He would *always* remember her voice and the comforting words she had imparted to him.

With a shrug, he shook away that fleeting sadness. He stood with Marilyn, the other refugees, and their armed guard escort at the railway line. The train tracks glinted dully in the early afternoon sun.

"Jom?" Hope tugged at his hand. "When's the train coming?"

"Soon, I think." Jom smiled at the girl. She had held onto him throughout the two-mile trek to the railway line. The journey had been uneventful though fear of another dalawg attack had never been far from everyone's minds.

The group he had joined was smaller than Jom expected it to be. After the dalawg attack, he thought more of the camp members would leave the stockade, but most had decided to stay.

Except those with him now. Isaac, a bearded man of middle years, his wife Ellen, and their two small children. A young woman named Alira, carrying her infant child, also accompanied them. All waited by the tracks, hoping to catch a ride on the approaching train. Isaac held a makeshift orange flag, part of an old blanket tied to a pole, to alert the train's engineer of their situation.

Jom glanced to his right, hearing the distant drone of the locomotive. Smoke billowing from the train's stack announced its eminent passage.

But would it stop for them?

Something flitted at the corner of Jom's vision. He looked to his right. There, in the distance, what looked like a very large bird dipped low and then vanished behind some nearby hillocks. Jom squinted. It was an odd-looking avian and the way it moved seemed unusual. Even the harpies Jom had observed were more graceful. Jom shrugged. During his captivity and travels afterward, he had seen more than enough strangeness.

And yet...

Sky Wolf alit behind a range of low hills close to the railway lines where the refugees had stopped. He climbed out and lay atop one of the hillock's crests. Directing his monocular toward where the refugees had stopped, he watched them. Once more earthbound, Torra now rumbled impatiently at his side. *You sense it too, eh?* Sky Wolf thought-sent. *One of the Outlander's locomotives approaches.*

The sound of a shrill whistle behind him confirmed Sky Wolf's guess. The train snaked into view, slowed, and stopped. The smell of burning coal and hot oil filled Sky Wolf's nostrils.

He focused his gaze and found himself enjoying the exuberant reaction of the girl-child.

"Here it comes!" Hope cried, jumping up and down.

As Isaac waved the orange flag, the train's whistle sounded. That was a good sign, meaning the train had room to shelter them, that those aboard possessed some semblance of kindness and pity. Of humanity.

Still, would they allow *him* on board because of his broken appearance and Kuront tattoo? He had never worked up the courage to try this before. He held his breath. The train slowed down. It *was* going to pick up them up!

"Jom," Hope said suddenly. "I want you to take off your eyepatch. I told you I like you better without it."

Jom stared at the little powerhouse of a girl. How had he come to be with her? It was like she had accepted and taken him on, rather than the other way around. "Not yet," he replied, knowing revealing his disfigured eye would disturb some of the others. "Maybe later. Now, look at the train. Ain't it somethin'?"

The locomotive itself was black and sleek, its pistons turning the silver driving wheels effortlessly as it chugged toward them. Jom admired the machine's shining armor-plated carapace, reminding him of the "dragons" mentioned in a story he had heard once. Adding to the illusion, the locomotive belched smoke and fire and seemed to roar like a great beast. As the train pulled closer, he saw a blue cross emblazoned on the front of the locomotive below the train's name--the *Aesculapius*.

"It's beautiful! What does that cross mean?" Hope asked.

Jom had learned a little about trains and the rebuilding and protection of some of the war-damaged railway lines through his travels, in camps, and from other solitary refugees. Most of the knowledge he had gleaned of the world had come from those random, untamed sources. "It means this's a hospital train," he replied.

"Which is good," Marilyn added. "The doctors and nurses can see to your needs. I've seen this train before, and it's stopped more than once for us. Its name comes from an ancient god of medicine and healing."

The locomotive pulled slowly past the group before stopping. An open flatcar brought up the train's rear. The emergency ground-mobile some trains carried stood cabled, its four wheeled, metal chassis tied securely to the flatcar's surface.

But Jom's attention diverted to a railcar coupled two cars in front of the ground-mobile. A red-and-white-painted carriage, its doors slid open. A soldier of the Gaia Defense Coalition and a tall, slim, copper-skinned GDC nurse stood in the entrance. They let down a wooden ramp to allow the refugees entry.

As Isaac and the others voiced their tearful thanks, as they ascended the steps into the carriage, Jom hesitated.

"It's okay, Jom," Marilyn said gently. She touched his arm. Was she being kind or just anxious to be rid of him? Sometimes Jom could never be sure, old insecurities returning. "Sometimes you have to take a chance."

"Why…why ain't you gone back to your old life?" Jom asked.

Marilyn shrugged, a faraway look in her eyes. "Nothing left for me back there. My life's here now like most refugees."

Nothing left. Was there anything for Jom anymore, anywhere? Could it be any better or worse wherever he was?

"Bye, Marilyn. I'll miss you," Hope said, hugging the older woman.

"Bye, sweetie. I'll miss you too." Marilyn ran a hand over Hope's head.

"But I'll come back to visit, I promise!" Turning to Jom, Hope tugged at his arm. "Come on, Jom, let's go!"

Marilyn smiled and handed Jom a leather pouch. "This contains the letter Chetan wrote on your behalf, vouching for your character and describing what happened to you. We felt it necessary because of the tattoo. Most of us signed it in agreement."

Most of us... Jom took the pouch and frowned.

"I know what you're thinking," Marilyn said. "But Carmen signed it too and not just because she wanted you gone."

"Jom!" Hope cried impatiently. "Come on!"

"Besides, who'll take care of Hope?" Marilyn said with a chuckle. "You know she's never taken to anyone like she has with you. I think that's a good sign. Good luck."

"Tha...thank you, Marilyn." *Take a chance! A good sign!* His heart beating rapidly, Jom shook her hand and placed the pouch under his arm. He pulled the hood tighter about his head and, with Hope leading the way, stepped up into the car.

He turned at the last moment. "I woan forget you 'n the others, Marilyn. I promise."

Most of the refugees boarded one of the rear cars, including the boy and girl-child. The woman-leader and the two guards stayed behind, as the train pulled forward to continue its journey.

Sky Wolf frowned, putting away his monocular. What was he to do now? The sense of importance, more than of simple curiosity, that had directed him here, wavered. Torra's insistence still pulled at him. The cougar chuffed, staring at his human.

You want us to follow the locomotive? Sky Wolf questioned. Torra pawed at the ground, his tail slashing back-and-forth. *Ah, my brother, how I wish sometimes you could form your thoughts into words.*

In a few moments, the *Nightbird's* lifting steam-jets propelled it skyward.

Twelve

Private Locomotive *Lionheart*
Northern Ohio Fringe Lands
Toledo Railway Branch Line

Peter Stamatis stood atop the parlor-coach roof, scanning the sky for the much-overdue Lakota hunter. The sun beat down but intermittent breezes helped keep Stamatis relatively cool. Wisps of smoke from the *Lionheart's* stack drifted by, dissipating on the wind. The engineer kept the locomotive stoked and ready for quick departure per Stamatis' standing order.

After unsuccessfully trying to concentrate on some company paperwork, Stamatis changed from his suit into more comfortable trousers, linen shirt, and ankle-boots, then climbed the ladder from the parlor-coach coupling platform to its roof. Anyone seeing him from a short distance would have pegged him as much younger than his fifty-six years, tall with a fit, muscular physique evident beneath his clothes. As long as he didn't draw attention to his damnable artificial leg!

Though the prosthesis worked well, it was a constant reminder of unfinished business. Plus, the phantom pain of his injury had never really gone away. Despite Alberta's pleas, he refused any laudanum. The discomfort kept him focused. His impatience and anger grew as he watched the horizon in vain for any sign of Sky Wolf.

He hadn't seen Alberta since their 'conversation'. No doubt she'd holed up in the sleeper-car, drinking herself into a stupor. Damn her, anyway! She'd been drinking more and more lately, despite her comfortable life. Plus, she'd been challenging him on certain issues more frequently.

Never mind. In some ways he couldn't blame her, considering her terminal condition. He'd talk with her later. Perhaps he'd reveal his little secret with her then. That would certainly please her. Despite everything, he still loved her. After a fashion.

"Sir? Mister Stamatis?" Willem poked his head up over the roof of the parlor-coach, clinging to the side-ladder. "There's a message coming over the telemax."

Stamatis grunted and descended the ladder behind Willem to the coupling platform connecting the parlor-coach to the office car. They entered Stamatis' office, where the clattering of the telemax machine sitting on his desk had just ended. Willem pulled a sheet of facsimile-print off the telemax and handed it to his employer. "Ah," Stamatis said, perusing the contents. "It seems our *reliable* Lakota Hunter, as you referred to him, has abandoned his hunt."

Willem frowned, a rare display of emotion. "Sir?"

"As you suspected, one of my wilderness agents spotted Sky Wolf miles away from his target area. It seems he's following some refugees from the Fort Ottawa refugee camp toward the Toledo/Dennison railway line."

"How odd," Willem mused. "Do you have any idea, sir, why he would do that? Is it possible his targets are Shifters hiding among the refugees?"

"Hmmm. A good guess, but that wouldn't adhere to his usual practice." Stamatis pursed his lips. Then, "Fetch my pistol, Willem. And have the men get the flyer unshackled from the flatcar. I'm going out there myself to find out."

"Is that wise, sir?"

"Just do it! I'm tired of waiting."

The flyer was basically a revamped ornithopter. Stamatis had commiss-ioned a complete refitting and redesign of the craft after he'd purchased it from the military. The lifting jets had been replaced with newly-developed propellers positioned on each stationary wing. Other innovations, such as landing wheels rather than mooring skids, and a gasoline-powered engine had also been installed. With the help of his Tech-Mages, he had learned how to pilot the craft. The new specs allowed Stamatis' artificial leg to fit comfortably in the enlarged cockpit. More or less.

But comfort was the last thing on his mind.

The flyer's canvas cover had been removed, its locking cables unfastened, and the flyer itself pulled down a ramp to the ground. Stamatis' sat in the pilot-seat, strapping in, and adjusting a pair of goggles over his eyes.

"Get the *Lionheart* to the location coordinates we just received," he said to Willem, who didn't look at all happy about his employer's decision. A second telemax message had come through. Another of Stamatis' agents, assigned to keep Stamatis updated on any developments throughout the Fringe Lands, described the refugees boarding a hospital train called the *Aesculapius*. An ornithopter had been sighted ascending behind it as the train headed toward Dennison, the military train hub.

"Sir, I insist you reconsider…"

"What in God's name is that Indigene up to?" Stamatis muttered, ignoring his aide.

"I could ask you the same question, darling." Alberta appeared on the opposite side of the flyer, garbed in her aviator's outfit.

"What are you doing?"

"I'm coming with you," she stated flatly, a single gloved hand resting on her hip. The other hand fingered a holstered pistol.

Stamatis laughed. "Like hell you are." With a passenger seat up front because of the wider space, Alberta had often flown with her husband. He had begun showing her how to use the controls. But this would be no joy ride.

In a quick, fluid motion, Alberta vaulted up into the passenger seat. "Let's go, love," she said, fastening her safety webbing. "Why should you have all the fun?"

Despite himself, Stamatis smiled. He reached for the control panel and started the engine.

Thirteen

Hospital train *Aesculapius*

"Yes, Matron," Nurse Kingbird said through the speaker-tube. "We're getting the refugees settled in the Staff Carriage until we reach Dennison."

"Good. Thank you, Audra. I shouldn't be too long. When I get back, do try to get some rest." Nurse Kingbird had returned to work after lunch, volunteering so Miriam could talk to the woman Songetay had singled out.

As the *Aesculapius* jerked once more into motion, Miriam replaced the Lounge Car speaker-tube and stifled a sigh. Bless the engineer for stopping the train to pick up those poor wretches! Audra had told her three children and an infant were among them.

Despite the recent victories and subsequent gains made by the GDC against the Eelees, the situation remained one of a stalemated nature. Neither side had proven to be the superior though it had taken a few years for the humans to get over the initial Eelee attack and marshal their forces. With a mutual enemy to fight, the Indigene nations had joined the fray, contributing to the defense against the invaders, particularly at the Battle of Horned Run. Still, a constant stream of displaced refugees and misguided distrust and aggression against them continued. Carriers of disease, some said, wild and uncivilized, a danger to civilized folk.

Sometimes Miriam doubted if people would *ever* be able to trust and help one another again.

The *Aesculapius*'s spacious, curtained, and carpeted Lounge Car, located at the middle of the carriage-line, contained a handful of soldiers whose injuries were less severe. Two had broken limbs which were set in slings or casts. Three nursed cuts and bruises, lying back against the headrests of their seats to nap, read, or gaze out at the passing landscape.

A group of four sat at small wooden tables near the windows, playing cards, smoking cigarettes, drinking coffee, which the train's galley crew served up along with other simple fare. A man and woman talked quietly, hands touching, perhaps hoping for another, more intimate, kind of respite from the war.

Miriam nodded and smiled to those who acknowledged her. Two of Lieutenant Camden's men greeted her as they mingled with the patients. She was a reassuring figure aboard the hospital train. Because of her own personal tragedy, Miriam could relate to and understand many of her patients' despondent attitudes.

At least, she always felt she could.

At the opposite end of the Lounge Car, a lone woman, a girl really, sat in one of the observation chairs, staring aimlessly out of the window. Dressed like the other soldiers in her blue GDC military uniform, she had taken off her tattered jacket, revealing a thin torso beneath a thread-bare shirt. A rolled-up sleeve exposed a cast on her right arm. To Miriam, she seemed to be far, far away, not sitting there in front of her at all.

Yet, for some reason, Miriam thought her own son, Arden, her Baby Boy, would be about Private Corson's age. Had he lived.

Corson. Interesting. Miriam hadn't noticed her before. She always made it a point to familiarize herself with the passengers aboard the *Aesculapius*. Not that Corson looked any different from any of the others—short brown hair, a haunted look on her pale face. She hadn't been treated on the train, of that Miriam was certain. Still, somehow, she'd slipped by Miriam's notice.

"Private Thelma Corson?" she asked. The girl stirred as if waking from a deep sleep and turned an anguish-filled look toward Miriam.

My God, Miriam thought, shocked at the depths of despair reflected in those pale eyes. *What has happened to her?* Such personal pain wasn't unfamiliar to Miriam. She had seen all manner of physical and mental damage during her tenure with the GDC. But the torment reflected in someone so young hinted at something more insidious.

"I'm Miriam Kosanavic," she said, regaining her composure. "I'm the Patient Liaison for the GDC and Nurse Matron of the *Aesculapius*. I do apologize for not introducing myself and seeing to your needs earlier. Is there anything you require?"

"Re...require?" The girl's voice, soft and high-pitched, struggled to escape her lips. A slight accent underlined her words, one Miriam couldn't place.

"Yes. I understand you haven't had anything to eat or drink since you've been aboard. Would you like some refreshment?"

"That is…very kind of you," Corson replied slowly, looking away. "But what I require cannot be consumed."

Interesting choice of words. "Spiritual advice then? Our chaplain couldn't be with us on this trip but I may be able to help you if you'd like to talk. I assure you all will remain confidential between us."

The girl's hands clenched the chair armrests, her knuckles turning white. "I wish to be free," she whispered. "To be away from this war, the killing. It is not right. Not right, no matter what we are told."

"No," she replied as gently as she could. "It's not right but we're only defending ourselves, aren't we? The Eelees attacked us first after the Veil fell, upsetting the balance of the Numinous Expanse."

Corson leaned back, closing her eyes. "Yes," she said. Then, she sat upright, once again facing Miriam. "Did you know some of the…*Eelees* can shift their shapes?"

It had been discovered a handful of Eelees existed which possessed certain unique abilities. Shifters, as they were called, were one such. "Of course," Miriam said.

"A group of them entered our camp, disguised as human soldiers, and slaughtered everyone." Corson licked her lips. "Except me. I managed to escape. It was my first…encounter with the enemy."

"How awful. I'm so sorry, Private." *She's not telling the whole truth,* she reasoned, relying on her nurse's training in reading body language and grasping the true meanings behind spoken words. Could she be experiencing what had been dubbed 'survivor's guilt'? *I suffered through that horrible stage myself. Could she be a deserter? She might just be faking a mental breakdown to escape the conflict.*

A condition Miriam had seen before with other war-weary soldiers. She'd encountered one man who, it was later discovered, had deliberately injured himself to get out of his military service. It wasn't her job to judge, though, and Miriam didn't begrudge anyone trying to survive any way they could.

The faces of her long-dead family appeared briefly in her mind. She and her dogs, Tar and Pitch (long-since passed on as well), had barely escaped the horror that had befallen her husband and son on the Day of the Collapse.

"I did not know it would be like that," Corson continued, interrupting Miriam's momentary, sad, reverie. "I did not know killing could be so…so…"

Again, something odd in the girl's choice of words and manner-of-speaking struck Miriam. "Like what, Private? What didn't you know?"

A braying sound like that of a maddened bull erupted throughout the Lounge Car. The warning klaxon! Startled, Miriam rose to her feet.

Behind her, those soldiers who were the most mobile also stood, directing their confused and fear-etched gazes toward the windows. Which quickly turned to anger accompanied by curses and shouts of rage. Miriam turned back, her eyes widening at the sight outside the Lounge Car.

Two eight-legged, spider-like creatures ran with blinding speed over the rough ground alongside the transport. Riding atop the monstrosities known as Spindlers sat their tall, thin, reptilian masters.

No, Miriam thought, memories burning. *Not again*.

With greenish-blue skin covered in scales, the riders' heads looked like a hideous combination of snake and human. Besides possessing arms and legs, a single coiling tentacle sprouted from each wide shoulder. Garbed in loose-fitting trousers and vests, the creatures each held a buzz-pistol in a clawed hand, using the other to grip the bony ridge rising behind the Spindler's skull.

Eelees. The *Aesculapius* was under attack by Eelees! It was those Lieutenant Camden had spoken of, surely, the Kuront survivors that had escaped the airship *G.A.U. DragonEye*. Immediately, the sharpshooters on the surveillance-sheds opened fire.

Miriam stifled a scream and turned back to the milling soldiers. "Calm down, please, everyone!" she cried, not totally convincing, even to herself. "The guards will handle this."

"Git us our guns!" one man shouted.

"Yeah!" another cried. "Let us fight those slimy bastards!"

"Stand down, soldiers!" Lieutenant Camden bellowed from the open door at the rear of the car. He stood on the car's deck near the coupling platform, revolver in hand, his dark-skinned features grim. "The Matron's right. My men will take care of it." As his two troopers took up positions at each end of the Lounge Car, Camden nodded approvingly at Miriam, and closed the door.

Miriam started at a sight to her left. She turned to see a third mounted Eelee on the opposite side of the Lounge Car. How many of the creatures were attacking the train?

Just then, as the single Eelee directed its nightmarish mount closer, the rider's head exploded in bone fragments, shredded skin, and splattering green ichor. A cheer arose from the wounded soldiers. Its master slain by the GDC marksmen, the Spindler lost all control and slid to a crashing, tumbling halt to its back, its hairy legs flailing above it.

A flash of blue iridescence lit up the Lounge Car windows on Miriam's side. Constructed of thick glass and clear diamonite, the pane withstood the buzz-pistol's blast while armor plating protected the body of the car. When the energy mist cleared, Miriam saw one of the two Eelees and its mount were also down. The third alien moved closer, maintaining its position alongside the Lounge Car, frantically urging its Spindler on.

It raised its weapon again, pointing it directly at the window where Miriam stood. The alien was so close now Miriam could see the sunlight reflected in those huge, faceted eyes. It opened its mouth, a long serpent tongue flicking. Once again, the rooftop marksmen found their target as the Eelee's chest caved in, the bullets knocking it backwards off the Spindler, its tentacles flapping. As with the others, the Spindler collapsed, devoid of its rider's control.

Miriam barely heard the accompanying hurrahs from the soldiers. She had turned away from the window to check on Private Corson. The girl sat huddled in her seat, knees drawn up to her chest, her face etched in fear. "Keep them away from me," she muttered. "Do not let them get me."

The alarm ceased, the silence jarring. Lieutenant Camden entered the car, announcing the danger was over. Instinctively, Miriam reached out to comfort Corson and covered the girl's hand with her own.

And pulled back in surprise. The girl's skin was so cold, like ice, like...

Nurse Kingbird suddenly appeared at her side, looking as shaken as Miriam felt. *No rest for the weary today*, Miriam thought. "Audra," she said, selfishly thankful for the interruption. "What is it?"

In response, Audra bent close to whisper in Miriam's ear. "I'm sorry, Matron, but some of the speaker-tube lines between cars were damaged in the attack. It's Sergeant Parker. She's convulsing violently. Dr. Songetay needs our assistance."

"Of course." Miriam rose, turning toward Corson. "Please excuse me, Private. I'll return shortly to continue our conversation but rest assured the threat is past."

As Miriam and Audra exited the Lounge Car, Miriam looked back, an inexplicable chill running up her spine. The patients celebrated the destruction of the Eelees, laughing, embracing, and clapping each other on the back. But Corson had stood up and stared after Miriam, her uninjured fist clenched at her side.

Fourteen

Hospital train *Aesculapius*

"Everyone, stay put!" the GDC soldier shouted above the wailing of the klaxons. Drawing his sidearm, the man exited the carriage. The door closed behind him, leaving Jom and the other refugees alone in what appeared to be the car where the medical staff slept.

Isaac went to the door and looked out its small window, tugging on his beard thoughtfully. "That soldier's climbin' up to the roof of the car in front us," he said, turning back with a puzzled expression. "Why're the alarms goin' off?"

"What's happening, Jom?" Hope asked. Both he and the girl sat on a bench set against the wall at the rear of the car. The rest of the refugees, except for Isaac, sat or lay on the staff cots.

At that moment, gunshots barked overhead and to the sides of the train. Jom rose and, with the others, turned to the carriage side-windows as Isaac pulled the curtains aside.

A collective gasp arose from the group. Toward the middle of the train, mounted Kuronts fired energy weapons from the backs of their thought-controlled dalawgs.

A sudden urging possessed Jom. He felt he was about to jump out of his skin. He had to get out and see what was going on! Handing Hope the leather pouch, he picked her up and set her down next to Alira. Alira pulled back at Jom's nearness, clutching her blanket-wrapped infant tightly. "Please," he said to the young woman. "Watch Hope for me."

"I'm not afraid of the Eelees, Jom," Hope said, clutching the pouch, her head held high. "But don't leave. I don't want you to be hurt."

"I'll be okay. You stay here."

What Hope said next stopped Jom cold. "I already lost my mama and papa." Sudden tears sprang to her eyes. "And I lost my voice. I don't want to lose you too. I...I want to sing for you."

He touched Hope's cheek, realizing they were both orphans, that they both needed each other now, that he wanted to hear her sing more than anything. "I'll be right back," he said, his voice quivering. "I promise."

Alira leaned close, her expression softening. "Go ahead," she said. "I'll watch her."

"Thanks." Jom squeezed Hope's hand and stood. He walked to the Staff Carriage door and pressed the square metal plate he had watched the soldier and the nurse activate. The door slid open.

"Hey!" Isaac shouted. "What're you doin'?"

Jom stepped out onto the connecting walkway, the coupling platform, between cars. Though a railing lined both sides, the platform lay open and uncovered, the countryside rushing by. He grabbed the railing, suddenly dizzy, and pushed himself forward to the next car.

He stood on shaky legs in front of the door, his eyes closed. He heard voices from the rail car he faced, shouting, tremors of fear in the words. Whoever was inside could be in trouble. He could help. Just like he did with Hope, he knew he could! He was human! These were his people! The memories of his First Life empowered him to act.

He couldn't, wouldn't be afraid this time. He pressed the entry plate on the car.

A Demon attack!
Sky Wolf guided the *Nightbird* to descend. Wind whipped against him, his braid flung out behind him. Three Demons had attacked the locomotive and been easily repulsed by the train's rooftop gunmen.

A desperate, useless action by the Demons, he thought. *Why?*

He changed course as an idea sparked. Was this assault simply a diversion? A delaying action of some kind? He had seen such desperation before. Utilizing the *Nightbird's* wing-cranks to lift him higher and faster, he soared over and past the locomotive. He watched the terrain ahead and below as he swiftly left the train behind, its smoking frame shrinking in the distance.

Torra screamed at the sight before them. The railway line ahead curved around a tall, rocky bluff, the tracks beyond it hidden. Sky Wolf's higher vantage point revealed two spider-mounts, directed by their Demon riders, had been harnessed to, and pulled, a large object onto the tracks.

A cannon-like weapon of the Demons, what the Outlanders called a "Blue-Fire Blaster." Damaged by the looks of it, the weapon would still block the railway line. The train would have no warning and, with this stretch of track and the Blaster concealed by the bluff, slam into the huge mass of twisted metal.

The locomotive and its cars would derail.

One of the Demons looked up. Shrieking in its unnatural voice, it raised a hand weapon to point at the *Nightbird*. Sky Wolf yanked the control-lever down and to his left. The 'thopter's banking-gears squealed at the sharp, abrupt maneuver, the wing cables stretched taut.

Reversing course, he flew the *Nightbird* back toward the oncoming train.

Guided by the flyer's built-in compass, Stamatis flew west toward the coordinates indicated in the telemax information. They were close. A few miles ahead, a column of smoke trailed horizontally across the horizon.

The hospital train *Aesculapius*. But where was Sky Wolf?

"Darling." Alberta broke his concentration. She leaned in from the right, her lips close to his ear. "What's really going on?"

He glanced at her. Alberta's expression beneath her goggles registered nothing. The ends of her scarf flapped in the wind. Faintly, a smell of bourbon clung to her breath. "What do you mean?" he asked, though he suspected the answer.

"Did you really think you could keep the real reason behind these hunts from me?" She smiled now, but one devoid of any warmth. "I got Willem to confess a little. You know how persuasive I can be. He didn't tell me everything, you'll be glad to know, but it was enough to see it's not to help the war effort. At least, not completely. You've never been that charitable."

"Alberta..."

"Oh, I know. You've registered with the GDC and have sent some information to their laboratories. All that looks good on paper and legitimizes the hunts, but there's something else, isn't there?"

"Yes," he said. Willem had been right, damn him! Peter needed to tell her. "It's for us. For you."

"What?"

He kept his attention on the sky ahead. He had to speak louder above the roar of the engine. "You know some Eelees can change their appearance."

"Shifters. So?"

"There are also those that possess strong, almost miraculous, healing powers."

"I've heard that. That they can fix their own kind's injuries, no matter how severe."

"If we can figure out how they do that, then maybe we can apply that information to humans. To us. Or maybe they *can* heal humans. We don't know. You can be cured. I can get my leg back. I didn't want to tell you until we got solid proof. I didn't want you to be disappointed."

Alberta stared.

"Before I hired Sky Wolf, we captured a Renegade Eelee and interrogated it. It spoke English. But all we got from it was these 'Healers' possess a different chemical makeup, something in that green ichor that passes for blood. There's nothing really on the surface that identifies them as such. Even the Eelees don't know exactly what makes these Healers different."

"And?"

He smiled, despite himself. She knew him too well. "With that knowledge, imagine the price we can get for it. The power."

Alberta leaned in, gently turned his head, and kissed him. "Thank you, darling," she said. "For a minute, I was afraid you really were about to turn benevolent."

"Only for us, my dear. Only for us."

A whistle blared ahead. The hospital train surged forward. Closer now, Peter saw a winged shape flying back toward the *Aesculapius* at a very low altitude. Alberta looked in the view-scope mounted on the control panel. "It's Sky Wolf," she said. "But there's something on the tracks ahead of him and the train."

A pause. "Eelees." Alberta squeezed Peter's thigh. "Let's go get them, love. Let's collect our own trophies."

Fifteen

Hospital train *Aesculapius*

It was worse than what Nurse Kingbird had described.

Sergeant Hannah Parker thrashed in the throes of a violent convulsion. Dr. Songetay stood over the young woman who lay in a top bunk, attempting to restrain her. "Matron!" he called out as Miriam and Audra rushed into the Infirmary Car. "Ready a hypodermic of morphine and *lorium*. Nurse Kingbird, help me hold her down!"

"What's happenin' to her?" Corporal Vega cried, sitting up in his own bunk. "What's goin' on?" Thankfully, the other patients still lay unconscious.

With practiced speed and precision, Miriam unlocked the medicine cooler, extracted the two tranquilizers, filled the large, glass syringe with the required dosages, and raced to Parker's bunk. Audra barely restrained the woman's kicking legs while Songetay held tightly onto Parker's wrists, facing her and leaning over her. The sergeant's torso heaved. Her head swung back and forth against the pillow with her mouth open in a silent scream.

"Quickly, Matron!" the doctor ordered through gritted teeth.

The Infirmary Car shuddered violently as if struck. Instantly, Miriam and her two colleagues were thrown off-balance. She and Audra stumbled back away from the bunk beds. Parker wrenched free of Songetay' loosened grip and lashed out at the doctor, her fist clipping him on the jaw. Already unsteady because of the car's violent motion, the doctor slammed into a set of bunkbeds and slid to the floor.

The car lurched again. The syringe flew from Miriam's hand as she fell back against the surgery cubicle. Parker's convulsive strength was too much even for the three of them.

She called out to Nurse Kingbird who rose to her feet from where she'd fallen, "Get help, Audra! Quickly! Get Lieutenant Camden!" Audra nodded, her lips set in a grim line, and turned to leave just as the door to the Infirmary Car opened.

Northern Ohio Fringe Lands

A s Sky Wolf drew closer to the train, he started in surprise. A sixth Demon and its spider-mount appeared as if from nowhere. They leaped out of concealment behind a group of boulders and threw themselves in front of the train.

The cowcatcher took the brunt of the collision, spearing and pinning the creatures beneath it. The locomotive rolled over the Demon and its mount, crushing them and splattering their remains. But though the locomotive remained intact and on-track, the great conveyance shuddered. Its entire carriage-line shook dangerously with the impact.

The Demons were doing everything they could to slow the train down, trying to make more time to completely block the tracks ahead. But for what purpose? What could be so important for them to sacrifice their lives for?

No time to think of that now. Sky Wolf angled the *Nightbird* and changed course once again. He dipped lower and flew abreast of the engineer's cab. The engineer gawked from the cab porthole at the winged craft pacing him. At the strange sight of a goggled Indigene piloting it and its feline passenger.

Sky Wolf pulled the ampli-phone from its control panel sconce and pushed its activator button. "Stop the train!" he cried in English, directing his words into the corded, palm-sized rectangular device. Like that of the Great Mystery himself, his voice boomed into the air from the front speaker-tube. "Tracks blocked ahead!"

In response, a gunshot roared from his right.

Hospital train *Aesculapius*

P rivate Thelma Corson stepped into the Infirmary Car from the coupling platform. "I heard the nurse describe the woman's distress," she said, her eyes cold and unblinking, her voice oddly slurred. "I am unique. I can help her. I can help all of them."

"Private!" Miriam said, taking a step toward her. "You can't be in here." Either oblivious to Miriam's entreaty or not caring, Corson swept up to Miriam and took her wrist in a vise-like grip. "No!" Miriam cried, struggling to pull away.

"I will help them," Corson repeated. "Please, do not interfere." She released Miriam and moved toward the bunk beds.

Recovering from her own surprise, Miriam shouted at a confused-looking Audra. "Go! Get Camden!" The young nurse turned and fled through the Infirmary Car door towards the Supply Carriage.

"Stop!" Songetay cried, struggling to his feet. With surprising strength, Corson stiff-armed the doctor back away from the bunks as easily as if Songetay were made of straw. Once again, Songetay fell and, this time, hit hard. His head bounced off the floor and he lay still, eyelids fluttering. Corson stood over Parker and, right in front of Miriam's astonished eyes, began to...*change.*

The private's body manifested into a blur of shivering motion, metamorphosing, growing, altering. Green, scaled skin ripped through her shirt and pants, her arm cast breaking apart. Her jaws elongated, her hair thinned and lengthened. The sickening sounds of crackling bones and rending tissue reached Miriam's ears. In place of the young private's girlish features, large yellow eyes and a wide split-of-a-mouth filled with needle teeth stared and gaped. A high-pitched clicking emitted from that long throat.

Tentacles uncoiled from her shoulders. Four of the undulating members, not two. Four!

"Holy Mother of God!" Corporal Vega cried. "I'd know that clickin' sound anywhere. It's a fuckin' Eelee!"

Miriam screamed. How was this happening? The thing that had pretended to be Private Corson unfurled one of its tentacles toward Vega. A second member wrapped around Sergeant Parker's head, and the third coiled about Lieutenant Hokatara's damaged leg in the bunk below Parker's.

Help them? My God, it's attacking them! Miriam looked around frantically. The unbroken syringe lay a few feet away. She scooped the hypodermic off the floor. "Stop it!" she cried, running toward the Eelee. "Stop it!"

The creature's fourth tentacle snapped out at Miriam like a whip, forcing her back as if she were a wild animal held at bay by its trainer. Miriam shouted in frustration, dodging the vile appendage. Then she stopped and, despite herself, gawked in amazement.

The creature's body trembled. A wavering glow emanated from its tentacles, flowing like St. Elmo's fire into the three patients.

What was it doing?

Then, as if that uncanny sight wasn't enough, a hoarse voice cried out. There, next to a reviving Songetay, knelt a viciously scarred boy. Clothed in oversize shirt and pants, he held a deformed, three-fingered hand out toward the Eelee. Once again, he spoke, his strange, foreign words accompanied by...clicks and whistles.

Entranced, Miriam watched as the Eelee's strange glow diminished, the alien disengaging its tentacles from the patients. It turned toward the boy and spoke as if replying to him.

The boy responded in turn with, once more, the Eelee answering. They were communicating.

"The...they're two of 'em now!" Vega shouted between gasping breaths. "God help us!"

Once more, the faces of Miriam's husband, John, and her son, Arden, flashed through her mind. "No!" she cried, taking advantage of the creature's distraction, unmindful of the rage mounting within her. She had never seen an Eelee up-close since that horrible day seven years ago. Though she had long ago suppressed any desire for revenge, the yearning to make the Eelees pay for her family's tragedy exploded.

"You evil, godless monster!" she shouted, moving now as if controlled by another, by her basest emotions. She lunged forward, holding the hypodermic above her head, ready to plunge it like a knife into the Eelee's putrid flesh.

The young boy stepped between her and the Eelee, open palms held before him. His already distorted features twitched. Miriam pulled back, her breath quick and ragged. "What are you doing?" she cried.

"Please, stop," the boy said. "The Kuront ain't bad. She's jes tryin' to help."

Though the boy's voice sounded impaired, something familiar about it, something in its tone and inflection, stirred Miriam's memory. But before she could react, the Eelee threw its head back and screamed. Its tentacles writhed above and around it like maddened serpents.

The Eelee lurched forward, knocking the boy aside. One of its tentacles struck Miriam in the shoulder, shoving her sideways. The alien hobbled away from the beds and fell to its knees. The green ichor that passed for its kind's blood trickled from its head.

"That'll fix it!" Corporal Vega stepped into view, his bandages torn from his face and hanging about his neck. He held his bloodied thumper-club in a white-knuckled hand. "Where's the other one?"

"Corporal?" Miriam stared at Vega. His eyes looked clear and free of injury. How could that be? "Your eyes!" Vega blinked, confused, and touched his face. Gently, Miriam took the weapon from him. Behind the private, Songetay rose to his feet.

"No, no!" The boy ran and knelt at the creature's side. Again, the two seemed to converse. As if instructed, the boy reached into the pocket of what was left of Corson's pants and took something from inside it.

The creature turned its reptilian gaze towards Miriam. As its tentacles dropped limply to the floor, slowly and painfully, it spoke. "They... The Kuronts, came for *me*." Its voice was low and sibilant, edged by a strange, clipped accent, much like...Private Corson's. "I rejoice in not going back." As its eyes flickered shut, the Eelee coughed and fell, whether senseless or dead, Miriam couldn't discern.

Lieutenant Camden rushed in, revolver drawn, two of his men right behind him with Nurse Kingbird bringing up the rear. The boy rose and backed away. "What the hell?" the lieutenant sputtered.

"Matron! Are you hurt?" Audra rushed to Miriam's side.

"No," Miriam said, feeling just as baffled. She lay the thumper-club on the bunk above Vega's. "I...I'm fine."

"What happened? Where did that Eelee come from?" Camden demanded "Where's Private Corson? Nurse Kingbird told us she was here."

"She... Corson *was* the Eelee."

"What? My god. A Shifter?"

"That boy," Miriam said, pointing. "Is he one of the refugee group we took on?"

Audra looked behind her. "Yes," she replied with a frown. "Why is he here?"

"Miriam, Audra." Both women turned. Dr. Songetay stood beside Sergeant Parker's bunk. The doctor's headband had been knocked off, causing his hair to tumble about his shoulders. The look on his face was one Miriam had never seen before. Awe? Bafflement? Both?

Corporal Vega still stood from where he had struck the Eelee. He rubbed his eyes, tears coursing down his cheeks. "Matron, Nurse," he said with a brilliant smile. "You're both as beautiful as I imagined. I can see. I can see!"

With a soft cry, Audra ran to the corporal as Miriam joined Songetay. Her hands trembled. "Doctor. Are you all right?"

"I'm fine. Look," Songetay said, indicating Sergeant Parker. Miriam stared, incredulous. Hannah Parker lay there, alert and aware, no longer comatose. "Where am I?" she asked hoarsely, licking her dry, cracked lips. "Is this a hospital train? Why am I bandaged up?"

As Songetay examined and talked to Parker, Miriam shook herself and knelt to the lower bunk to see to Lieutenant Hokatara. Immediately she saw the man's skin had regained some color, his breathing had become more regular. Though the faint stink of gangrene still lingered from his amputation, Miriam suspected what she would find.

Fetching a pair of scissors, she carefully cut the bandages around the wounded soldier's leg. Even as she watched, the black filth of the gangrene faded from the stump, replaced by healthy, pink skin.

Like magic. Like a miracle.

She stood up, feeling as if she were floating. Songetay gently took her arm and guided her away from the beds as Vega and his sergeant greeted each other ecstatically. Audra's face filled with wonderment, tears welling in her eyes.

The refugee stood apart, watching, as Lieutenant Camden and his men surrounded the Eelee. Again, Miriam felt something familiar about the boy.

"Onta," Miriam turned back to Songetay, knowing she was grasping at straws, trying to rationalize what had just happened. It had been reported some doctors and shamans had teamed up to try and create new healing techniques. "Was this you? Did you use your shaman powers to cause this...this phenomenon?"

"No, Miriam, it wasn't me. I don't have that kind of power on my own else I would have used it long ago." Songetay glanced to his right. "You saw it as I did. It was the Eelee."

The glow that emanated from the alien. She followed Songetay's spellbound gaze. Camden ordered his men to bind the Eelee. Capturing a live one had rarely happened during the war and would be quite an accomplishment for the GDC.

Miriam couldn't let that happen. At least not yet. She cast a questioning look at the refugee boy. "The Honored Fem ain't dead," he said, understanding. "Jes knocked out." He meant the Eelee—the Kuront, the Demon, the being—that had masqueraded as Private Thelma Corson; the being that had cured Vega, Parker, and Hokatara; the being Miriam and Vega had almost killed.

"Lieutenant," she said to Camden. "Please, have your men put the Eelee on the table in the surgical cubicle."

"Matron?"

"It...*she* needs medical attention."

"What?" Camden shot a confused glance at Songetay.

"Yes," the doctor said, placing a hand on Miriam's shoulder. "Matron Kosanavic is correct."

"Now wait a minute..."

"This has become a medical issue," Miriam continued, drawing herself up. "The Eelee treated our patients, healed them, in fact. Look for yourself. As such, we have seniority in this matter and must reciprocate."

Camden sputtered. "How the hell would you even know how to treat it?"

Miriam glanced at the refugee. "I believe we have someone here who could help us with that."

"Lieutenant," Songetay said. "Please do as the Matron says."

At that moment, the train whistle sounded. The *Aesculapius* slowed, jerking, its breaks screeching. No time to wonder why, Miriam knew. Right now they had work to do.

Sixteen

Northern Ohio Fringe Lands

A bullet careened off the *Nightbird's* diamonite-laced fuselage. Sky Wolf veered away and up from the train. One of the locomotive's defensive sharpshooters took aim again from a rooftop surveillance-shed.

Torra screamed his agitation.

"I am not your enemy!" Sky Wolf cried, the speaker-tube broadcasting his desperate plea. "Tracks are blocked ahead! Stop the train!"

He dropped closer, repeating his message. The sharpshooter hesitated as another soldier's head popped up over the end of the car. Hanging onto the car's side-ladder, the man shouted at the sharpshooter who nodded and lowered his rifle. The engineer stared, then reached his hand over his head.

The locomotive's whistle blew, echoing another of Torra's screams. Sparks flew from the train's squealing wheels as the train braked. Putting the ampli-phone down, Sky Wolf waved and pointed ahead.

As the train ground to a juddering halt, the Lakota Hunter soared toward what he hoped were the final two Demons. He squinted. What was this? In the distance near the blocked track, another flying craft descended.

What the hell?

Stamatis soared above two Eelees and their cursed spindlers. Two were using the spider-beasts to pull a damaged Blue-Fire Blaster onto the tracks, hidden behind a tall bluff. He reasoned Sky Wolf had flown back to warn the oncoming train.

A chill gripped Stamatis, a compulsion he had long tried to control.

The Eelees had maimed him in an attack on one of his factories two years earlier. That same assault had seriously wounded Alberta. It wasn't enough his factory armaments helped the GDC military to kill the invaders. Here was a chance for him and his wife to exact revenge directly. Personally. As Alberta had said—to get their own trophies.

He wanted them dead!

He dropped the flyer lower and pulled out his pistol. Alberta laughed. He glanced to the side to see her readying her own gun. Banking the flyer to the right, he gave Alberta the position to open fire first. The Eelees slithered for cover behind the Blaster. Their spindlers hissed, rearing up.

"Let's get them, Peter!" Alberta cried gleefully. Stamatis grinned. It was as if both of their pain and anger had finally broken free. A killing lust erupted, civilization's façade slipping away. They should have done this a long time ago!

Stamatis flew past the bluff and began to turn back. As if God himself spoke, a voice boomed out of the air itself. "Stop! Don't attack them!" Sky Wolf! Using his onboard ampli-phone. The ornithopter flew parallel to him, the Lakota waving frantically. "Stamatis!" Sky Wolf cried, shocked recognition written on his face. "Back away! The Demons have weapons." His filthy animal, strapped in behind him, screamed in unison.

"The hell with you!" Stamatis shouted, raising his pistol. He fired at the Hunter, just missing his target as Sky Wolf jerked the 'thopter up and to the left.

"Forget him!" Alberta shouted, pointing below. "Go back for the damn Eelees!"

Stamatis continued banking, heading once more toward the blocked track. Yes, they'd kill those Eelees. They'd… A flash of blue light erupted from below. A hiss like a thousand snakes, a jarring vibration.

Alberta screamed. Stamatis cried out, the flyer rocking back and forth. The controls froze, the steering column stuck. Another flash of blue light. The flyer's engine squealed and the craft spun earthward. Stamatis struggled with the steering column. He looked to his right. The passenger seat was empty, his wife's webbing torn away.

'No, no, noooooooooo!" He thrashed in his seat, pounding his fists against the control panel. Smoke pouring from the craft's burning fuel enveloped him.

Sky Wolf watched in horror. Stamatis' flyer spun into the ground beyond the tracks. The craft's fuel ignited, exploding in a ball of fire.

A searing shock wave buffeted the *Nightbird*. Sky Wolf pulled up on the control-lever and ascended. His own anger sparked at what the Demons had done. Before he could act, sudden impressions flooded his mind. Torra. A sense of calm, of reason, emanated from the usually excitable cougar.

Now was not the time to lose control.

You are right, my brother, Sky Wolf thought-sent. His Outlander employer had tried to kill them. Who was the real enemy here? Whatever hatred drove Stamatis and his wife must not be repeated.

Hatred begat hatred, violence begat violence. It had to end.

Below, two of the Demons had untied and clambered onto their spider-mounts. The third lay burnt and twisted, too close to the downed flyer to escape the explosive blast. Its spider-mount limped away. A dust cloud kicked up by the fleeing Demons quickly faded in the distance. *They are in luck this day,* Sky Wolf thought. He circled the *Nightbird* to bring it earthward when more urgent impressions from Torra entered his mind. Sky Wolf started in surprise.

A survivor lay below.

Hospital Train *Aesculapius*

"*What do you do, Honored Fem? Why are you here?*"

"*You speak our tongue. Then know this, I pose no threat. I want, I need, to help the humans. To make amends for the part I have played in this misguided war. For too long I have been afraid, cowardly.*"

"*No, you helped us! That is not the act of a coward.*"

"*I hope that is true.*"

"*You...you are a Healer and a Shifter both.*"

"*Yes, one tired and sickened by conflict and death.*"

"*The others came for you?*"

"*To take me back or kill me. Because I possess a way to possibly help end the conflict. Those who attacked us belong to the war faction, who wish to continue fighting. Not all of us do. Not anymore.*"

The words spoken by the Kuront echoed in Jom's mind. The Kuront *scientist* had spoken of peace. But Jom had never heard of a Kuront who possessed the dual abilities of a Shifter and a Healer or one who harbored such a desire to rebel against its own kind. Jom felt a great sadness at the alien's injury yet he couldn't fault the man for hitting it, unique though the Honored Fem was. They had all been frightened and confused.

You are hurt, Honored Fem!

No matter. In the pocket of this garment…take the message-tube. I would have given it to those humans who would understand its significance. Those in command at the Dennison Depot. Now I may not be able to. You must take charge of it, see that it gets into the right hands.

Charge of it… The small metal cylinder given to him by the Kuront still lay in his clenched fist. He put it in his pocket, not understanding, wondering if he had now been given another burden, another responsibility, he would find too hard, too much.

He stood inside the surgery cubicle as the Indigene doctor and the Nurse Matron finished tending to the Healer. They had stopped the bleeding and dressed the Kuront's head wound. The Nurse Matron had asked Jom to watch, to…*advise* them on anything special regarding the Kuront's physical makeup. In the end, he didn't have to say much, but his gaze wasn't for the Healer anymore but for the Matron. He could barely take his eyes off the older nurse.

Her voice. He recognized her voice.

Now, as she exited the cubicle, leaving the doctor alone with their alien patient, Jom followed. The younger nurse stood at the bunk beds occupied by those the Healer had cured. The Matron turned as she wiped her hands with a damp cloth. She regarded Jom, her brow knitted questioningly. Jom went to her side and took her hand. Startled, the Matron looked into the one, clear, blue eye amidst all his ruined flesh.

"Mama," he said, pronouncing the cherished word he only uttered when he cried himself to sleep or woke from nightmares. It was a word he thought he would never use again in this way. "Mama. Mirrie."

The woman's eyes grew wide. She dropped the cloth and put her free hand to her chest. She tried to pull away, disbelief shadowing her startled gaze. But he held onto her, his grip strong, urgent, needy.

One of the GDC soldiers standing guard in the infirmary took a step toward them. The Matron waved him off. She blinked and then stepped closer to Jom. Slowly, she raised her hand and placed it tenderly against the broken side of his face. He trembled at her touch. She was older, but it was his mother. He knew it. So beautiful, so caring, her hand soft and warm. "My boy," she said softly. "Sweetheart. Arden. Is it really you?"

"Mama." His hoarse words barely made it through his twisted lips. Tears ran down his cheek. "I…I know your voice. I'd know it anywhere. It's me, Mama. Yer Baby Boy."

With a joyous cry, she folded him into her arms.

Seventeen

Northern Ohio Fringe Lands

Sky Wolf brought the *Nightbird* to a landing, positioning its skids in front of the bluff which concealed the wrecked Blaster. Unwebbing himself and Torra, he looked questioningly at his spirit-brother. *Show me,* he thought-sent.

Torra leapt out of his seat and loped toward a small depression in the ground a short distance from the tracks. Sky Wolf retrieved his medicine bag and followed his spirit-brother. The fierce heat of the burning flyer pummeled him.

Sky Wolf looked down as he strode past the fiery wreckage. An unnatural-looking object lay on the ground. Stamatis' burnt and blackened artificial leg.

Torra bounded into the depression, his tail erect. Sky Wolf slid down the side of the narrow, gully to find Stamatis' wife. Wrapped in torn safety-webbing, Alberta Stamatis lay on her back. Sky Wolf knelt at her side. She lived, though she was injured. Sky Wolf reasoned what remained of the webbing must have cushioned her fall.

Still, the woman had sustained injuries and needed help. Sky Wolf's own healing ability and talismans couldn't sufficiently treat such wounds. He needed to get her to the train. Just then, Torra pricked his ears. Short, sharp chugging sounds. Sky Wolf recognized them as emanating from an emergency ground-mobile most locomotives carried.

Stay with the woman, brother, he ordered. Sky Wolf rose to his feet and climbed out of the depression to meet those who approached. He held his arms at his side, open palms facing forward.

The ground-mobile stopped near the *Nightbird*, and four uniformed GDC soldiers, both men and women, got out. A nurse, an Indigene, also exited, carrying a medical case. At a word from a tall officer, two of the soldiers moved away to examine the Blaster, while one went to check on the burning flyer.

"Greetings, sister," Sky Wolf said with a short bow then pointed to where Mrs. Stamatis lay. "The woman is injured. My spirit-brother watches over her. He will not harm you, but I will accompany you, just the same." The nurse smiled and nodded as she rushed past.

Despite Sky Wolf's assurance, the nurse hesitated upon seeing Torra. Sky Wolf called the cougar away to allow the nurse to examine Mrs. Stamatis. He and Torra stood at the top of the depression where the officer, a black-skinned Outlander, joined them, carrying a stretcher.

Sky Wolf turned and studied the man, sensing intelligence and compassion about him. The soldier introduced himself, and appraised Sky Wolf thoughtfully. "A Demon Hunter who flies," he said, a sparkle dancing in his brown eyes. "And who keeps a white cougar as his spirit-brother." He looked at Torra. "Reckon I've seen it all now."

Sky Wolf cocked his head. This Lieutenant Josias Camden knew of his profession and seemed not-at-all disturbed by Torra's presence. Interesting.

"I fought at Horned Run," Camden said, as if reading Sky Wolf's thoughts.

"As did I," Sky Wolf replied. "I am Sky Wolf and this is Torra. We are pleased to meet a fellow warrior."

Camden held out his hand. Pausing only a moment, Sky Wolf extended his own, both men grasping forearms. Torra rubbed his side against Camden's long leg, giving his approval. Sky Wolf nodded, thinking he could be friends with this black man.

"Much obliged, Sky Wolf," Camden said. "It's not often I've heard of a Demon Hunter helping folks out. There's a lot of people here who'd like to thank you."

Sky Wolf grunted in reply, a sensation he hadn't felt in a long time running through him. A feeling, an emotion, akin to...*kinship*.

Camden looked toward the fiery remains of the flyer. "What can you tell me about that?"

Sky Wolf related what had transpired since he and Torra had arrived at the refugee camp during the dalawg attack. Leaving nothing out, he told of the Stamatis' hunts and Sky Wolf's interest in the boy.

"A scarred refugee boy?" Camden said. "Yep, he's on board the *Aesculapius*, all right. Funny thing about him..."

"Lieutenant?" the nurse called out. She still knelt at Alberta Stamatas' side, wiping her hands with a towel.

"Nurse Kingbird," Camden said. "What's her condition?"

"We have to transport her back to the Infirmary Car, Lieutenant.

She needs immediate attention for possible broken ribs, collar bone, and a concussion. It could have been worse though. I think the safety-webbing protected her from more serious injuries."

Without a word Sky Wolf and Camden slid into the depression with the stretcher.

After Mrs. Stamatis had been carefully bundled onto the ground-car, a soldier drove her and Nurse Kingbird back to the locomotive *Aesculapius*. Sky Wolf helped the GDC soldiers move the Blaster. It took a lot of brute strength and some creative leveraging, but the five of them were finally able to maneuver the weapon off the tracks. Sky Wolf's respect for Camden increased as the officer joined in the work, not content to allow those he commanded to simply do his bidding.

Yet, though much curiosity about him and Torra was evident in the way the soldiers looked at him and in the few questions Camden asked, most of the conversation Sky Wolf overheard centered on what had happened inside the *Aesculapius*.

Something important, it seemed. Something extraordinary. Something about a Demon who heals. *I must find out about this,* he thought.

Sky Wolf spoke briefly to Camden of his intention. Allowing Torra to lope back to the train, he lifted the 'thopter into the air. He glided close to the locomotive then landed near the front of the carriage-line before disembarking. He waited for Torra to catch up.

Is this the real reason you insisted I help those at the Fringe Lands' stockade? he thought-sent, locking eyes with the beast as he knelt in front of him. *To be here, now, at this place? With these people? It was never to simply lend assistance, was it?*

Torra chuffed and slowly blinked.

Ptesan-Wi has been working through you all along. Yes, my brother? Perhaps it was the White Buffalo Calf Woman herself who led me to you that day I found you. But why did you wait so long to reveal your true self?

Ptesan-Wi's words came back to him. *"Everything in its own time."*

Torra moved his sleek body into Sky Wolf's arms. His purring vibrated through the Lakota Hunter as Sky Wolf embraced him. *Then come, Torra. Let us follow this path to its end.*

They strode the length of the iron conveyance as its crew readied to continue its journey. Those passengers within stared at him and Torra through the cars' windows, some pointing. A few others stood on the coupling platforms, calling out their gratitude. The news had spread quickly, it seemed.

Near the end of the line, three figures waited outside of a red-and-white carriage. They watched Sky Wolf and Torra intently, their scrutiny more intense than the others. An energy, a compelling aura of resolve, of strength, resonated from the three. The scarred refugee boy, the girl-child from the Fringe-Lands stockade, and a GDC nurse walked forward to meet him.

He spoke to the nurse, who was not the one he had met at the blocked tracks. "The woman, Alberta Stamatis. How does she fare?"

"She's stable," the nurse answered. "We'll need to get her to the clinic at Dennison for further treatment but I think she'll recover." She paused. "Unless our other patient is well enough to treat her."

Sky Wolf frowned, not understanding her remark. Perhaps it had something to do with what he had overheard about the Eelee Healer.

"I know you," the boy broke in. "You shot the dalawg at the refugee camp, dint you? You saved Hope 'n me. Tha...thank you."

"Thank you!" the girl echoed.

"Yes," the woman added. "And thank you for warning the engineer. You saved us all."

Sky Wolf bowed his head, feeling...humbled? He stood before singular presences, he was certain. Three beings who harbored power, who were more than they seemed. Torra had been correct in leading him to the boy.

"All three of you have suffered," he said slowly, his spirit-bonded thoughts reaching out, touching them, feeling their pain. "Yet you have retained your true selves despite that suffering. That is something to be honored and respected. It takes courage beyond what most possess." *What I once had and lost.*

The boy looked down, his lips quivering. The woman put an arm around his shoulders. A bond existed between the two, perhaps a familial one. The girl, however, boldly stepped forward. "What's your cat's name?" she asked wide-eyed. "He's all white!"

Sky Wolf smiled. It was an act, he realized, which seemed long out-of-practice. "Torra. And I am Sky Wolf."

"I'm Hope!" she said enthusiastically. "And this is Jom, I mean Arden, and Miriam."

The cougar rose and approached her. For a moment, the nurse Miriam looked worried, reaching out to the girl.

"He will not harm any of you," Sky Wolf said.

Torra walked up to Hope and lowered his head. The girl patted him. "He's so soft!" she said. "And he's purring!"

"Torra has deemed you a friend, little one," Sky Wolf said, his smile growing. "He does not allow that with everyone."

The cougar then acknowledged Jom and Miriam in the same manner before returning to Sky Wolf's side.

"What will you do now?" Miriam asked.

"I have much to think about," Sky Wolf replied, realizing it was true. "My life and that of my spirit-brother have…changed."

"As have ours."

"Come with us!" Hope cried.

"Yuh," Arden added. "We kin…kin work together."

Work together. Those words held a certain appeal for Sky Wolf. But not yet. "We must go away for a while," Sky Wolf replied regretfully, knowing at that moment what he needed to do. "I must smoke the Sacred Pipe of *Ptesan-Wi* and reflect on my past actions. Perhaps someday Torra and I will return and join you then."

At that moment, the sound of a distant whistle pierced the air. Sky Wolf looked up as one of the hospital train's rooftop sharpshooters exited his surveillance-shed. He gazed through a pair of binoculars toward the north. "What is it, soldier?" Sky Wolf inquired.

The GDC trooper looked down. "Another train, running on the branch line about a half mile away," he said. "Its designation reads *Lionheart*."

Ah, Sky Wolf thought grimly. *Stamatis' train. One now without a master.*

Eighteen

GDC Military Railway Line Hub
Dennison, Ohio
Gaia American Union

Miriam had pledged her life to the GDC. Its members had taken her in, brought her back to sanity. They had helped her to overcome her grief and to regain her faith, giving her life a purpose once more. She had taken back her unmarried name, as a result, to further illuminate her new existence and to put the misery of the past behind her.

Now, against all reason, a precious part of her past had returned, changing her life yet again. Despite everything that had happened, an unbound joy rushed through Miriam. Her son. Arden was alive! She squeezed his hand to reassure herself she wasn't dreaming.

The afternoon sun shone brightly over Dennison in a cloudless sky. Smoke from the stacks of two troop transports spiraled upward above the depot building and train hub complex. Various military and civilian passengers disembarked and boarded the trains, the depot platform a whirl of bustling activity.

The Sisters of St. Mortimer were, as usual, greeting soldiers, directing them to the canteen, and dispersing all manner of welcoming cheer. The smells of baked goods wafted through the air.

Miriam, Arden and Onta Songetay sat on a bench in front of the Dennison Clinic, trying to rest before their interview with the local military authority. Per regulations, all the passengers aboard the *Aesculapius* would need to relate what had happened during the Eelee attack.

Several yards away stood the gentleman from the *Lionheart*, one Willem Vogt, the aide to the late armaments magnate, Peter Stamatis. His arms folded, his head down, he seemed lost in thought. He had been allowed aboard the *Aesculapius* to travel with Stamatis' wife, who had been rushed immediately into surgery upon their arrival at Dennison. Vogt gave no outward sign of emotion, perhaps resigned at the death of his employer.

The *Aesculapius* had been routed to the depot roundhouse, the locomotive spattered with gore and dirt. Workers would remove, clean, and disinfect the last traces of the ichor and Spindler blood, torn flesh and bones clinging to the front of the transport, the cowcatcher, the sides of its sleek, black frame, the engineer's cab, and smokestack. Steam-blasting the remains of the hidden Eelee attacker and its Spindler from the wheels, cranks, and cylinders would assure nothing would be left of the foul creatures.

The Eelees had, evidently, wanted their Shifter back very badly or, if that failed, stranded or dead. If not for the Lakota Sky Wolf and his amazing flying craft, many would have died.

Miriam, Audra, and Songetay had helped the patients off the train with Arden also lending assistance. The three most seriously injured soldiers had left under their own power. Hokatara used crutches, Vega and Parker walked together, arm-in-arm, rank and regulations be damned. Along with the refugee group, all were escorted to the clinic. Though those grievously injured had been healed, a follow-up examination had to be made.

Audra Kingbird had stood muttering under her breath then, a glazed look in her eyes. It had sounded like she was praying. *Was it a miracle?* Miriam pondered again. *A twisted working of some unfathomable deity?*

Like her son. Arden was alive but what kind of person had he become after all the suffering he had experienced? A prisoner of the Eelees and who knew what else! Why did he have to go through that? Perhaps more disturbing, she had almost killed an innocent being, one who had been trying to help them. Had she succeeded, how would she have lived with that fatal action?

Songetay gently touched her arm. "Miriam?" he asked again. "Are you all right?"

"Why would God allow this?" she said softly. "All this death and destruction? This insanity?"

Songetay nodded. "I don't know if we'll ever know the answer to that," he said. "*Gitchi-Manitou*, my people's Great Spirit, works in much the same inexplicable ways. Yet here we are."

"It, *she*, was a deserter," Miriam said.

"Yes," Songetay replied. "Ironic, isn't it? Renegade Kuronts are basically deserters too, though they shun human society as well as their own."

"She saved them." Miriam's words caught in her throat. She wasn't sure if "ironic" was a strong enough word. "The Healer said she could help them but I thought she'd killed them. I didn't believe her."

"None of us did," Songetay put his arm around her. She started for a moment, then relaxed into his comforting embrace. "I thought she meant the patients harm as well."

"And I tol' you too late," Arden added. "Afore the soldier hit her. It's my fault too."

"No, no..." Miriam drew away from Songetay and took her son's hand. "It's no one's fault."

"The Healer will be taken into custody to be interrogated when she recovers," Songetay said. "Arden, I suspect they'll want you to help with that."

Miriam bristled. "We must see that she is not mistreated!"

"Lieutenant Camden will be in charge. He's a good man and he saw the results of the Healer's powers."

"She said she was unique, that's why the others who attacked the train wanted her back." Miriam shook her head, realizing with astonishment, despite seven years of war, they knew so little about their enemy. "Perhaps *that's* the reason," she continued. "Maybe we had to learn not all the Eelees are monsters. She didn't want to fight anymore. She would have rather hidden among humans then go back to her own kind. Don't you think that's remarkable?"

Songetay replied, "Eelee Shifters have infiltrated human settlements before. She could have been a spy or saboteur."

"But, Mama," Arden said, "Doctor, some of the Kuronts want peace. Some *do* wanna fight. That's the war...*faction*. But the Healer said others dint wanna fight no more. Like the Renegades and the scientist at the compound where I was a prisoner."

Arden suddenly bolted to his feet, his startled cry mingling with the final boarding whistles. Reaching into his pants pocket, he pulled out a small, tube-shaped object. "I forgot," he said. He showed the cylinder to Miriam and Songetay. She took it from his trembling hand.

A few inches long, made of a golden metal, the tube was covered in a type of writing, of raised symbols or glyphs. Miriam recognized them as the written form of the Eelee language.

"The Eelee," Songetay said, "the Kuront, gave this to you, Arden?"

"Yuh," Arden replied. "Right afore she passed out. She tol me it was a message-tube and has to go to people who'd understand it. She said for me to take charge of it."

"Yes," Miriam said. "I saw you take it from her but didn't know what it was."

"These symbols." Songetay ran a finger over the surface of the glyphs. "What could they mean? We've never been able to fully translate the Eelee language."

A message-tube. Miriam looked at her son, somehow knowing what he'd say next.

"I kin read it," Arden said.

"This says how to open the tube 'n get the message inside," Arden said, indicating the glyphs. "There's no danger, Doctor."

Still suspicious, Songetay had expressed concern the tube might be a weapon or an explosive device. But it wasn't Miriam this time who reassured him but Arden, who jumped at the chance to help.

"Can you open it?" Miriam asked.

"Yuh." Arden performed a quick action with his right hand, pressing the cylinder in three select spots. The top of the tube flipped up, revealing a small scroll within.

Miriam and Songetay sat with Arden at a table in the Depot's recreation hall. Lieutenant Camden stood behind them, having joined their group at Songetay' request. The hall was empty except for a staff member sweeping the floor at the opposite side of the large room, ensuring some privacy for the foursome. Before they approached the officials of the GDC Military Command, they all wanted to be sure what the mysterious cylinder contained.

Carefully, Arden removed the parchment, unrolled it, and perused the Eelee script written on its surface. Miriam reached out and carefully touched his arm, still not certain he was real, still afraid she'd awaken from a dream and he'd be gone. Beneath her fingers, she felt his body tremor.

Arden looked at her, wonder in his eye. "It's…" He paused, trying to find the correct word. "Instructions. It tells how the Dimen…the Dimen…"

"Dimensional Veil?"

"Yuh, yuh! How all the portals of the Dimensional Veil that's left kin be sealed up all the way. How we kin block the Eelee war faction from gittin' their supplies 'n weapons 'n set the Nu…Numinous Expanse aright. It woan…it woan be needin' anyone to be hurt or die neither like what happened at Horned Run. It's…it's Kuront *science*!"

Songetay muttered, invoking the name of his people's Earth-Mother spirit. "If this is so, and our Tech-Mages can make it work, it can change everything."

"Holy shit." Camden added his own, more earthy sentiment. "Uh, sorry, Matron, Doctor, Arden, but I reckon Command will want to see this all right."

"No need to apologize, Lieutenant," Miriam said, suppressing a cry of joy. She took hold of Arden's mutilated hand. "Arden," Miriam said softly, trying to keep her voice steady. "Are you sure?"

Arden nodded, his damaged face alight. Miriam knew what he and everyone else now thought. The Eelee Shifter wasn't a deserter or a saboteur.

She could very well be a savior.

Nineteen

Within the Vision-Realm of Ptesan-Wi

It was a dream like no other.

A dominion of light, of soft drumming, and the familiar sounds of flutes, whistles, and rattles. Of richly textured patches of earth, sky and water. The smells of baking bread, roasting meats, the laughter of children.

Once more Sky Wolf found himself in the Numinous, within the Vision-Realm. This time he was not afraid. This time, it was different.

He stood on the bank of a wide flowing stream, its crystalline waters sparkling. On the opposite shore, within a large open glade, sprawled an Indigene village. No *tipis* of his own nomadic Nation had been erected on that spot, but rather disparate lodgings of a more permanent nature. Longhouses, wigwams, earthen and plank structures, buildings of brick and stone, had been built into a very special community.

Children ran playing, adults watched laughing as they worked. Many were Lakota, Cheyenne, and of other Indigene Nations. There were peoples of the Eastern realms and white and black-skinned Outlanders. *How can this be?* Sky Wolf thought. *Such peace, such acceptance, such unity.*

A welcoming, invisible caress blanketed him. *I am home,* he thought in wonder. A presence sparked behind him, gentle yet strong. He turned again toward the White Buffalo Calf Woman, she who had guided his life since the Battle of Horned Run, though he had never known it. Braided hair, fringed, deerskin dress and tunic, and her blue eyes, so unlike those of other Lakota women…

Sky Wolf gasped, feeling as if he had been struck a blow. Blue eyes. No. The woman before him was not Ptesan-Wi!

"Tashina," he breathed. "Is it truly you?"

"It is, Mahpiya, beloved one." Like a star fallen to Earth, Tashina stood wreathed in light, holding a swaddled infant in her arms. The baby chirped, its little hands waving above it, as if in greeting. "And our son, Hotah."

Sky Wolf took a step toward her. "Hotah. Our son..."

"Please, Mahpiya, no closer." Tashina held out a warning hand. "Though it grieves me, if we touch, our connection, this moment we have now, will end. You must keep a distance."

"What cruelty is this?" Here, at long last, stood his beloved *mitawin*. Right in front of him! And he was forbidden to touch her? To hold her and their son?

Their son!

"Such is the way of the Numinous." Tashina smiled, that beautiful expression which had ever sent shivers of awe through Sky Wolf. Even when alive, she had always bespelled him with her intelligence, wisdom, courage, and beauty. Her shamanic abilities, though impressive, could never match the power of her inner light. How had he survived without her? "These things cannot be explained or understood, no matter how hard we try," she continued. "Ptesan-Wi has brought you here into the Spirit World so I can tell you this. Do not grieve for Hotah and me."

"How can I not?" Sky Wolf hungered to hold Tashina, to look into Hotah's eyes. Once more the way of the Great Mystery confounded him.

"We are safe and where we must be. You too are where you must be and must move onward. There is much more for you to do yet in the world of the living." Another smile. "It is your destiny, Warrior of the Air."

"Destiny again." Sky Wolf allowed himself a small smile. Once more his *mitawin*, even in death, calmed and reassured him. Gave him hope. "I am not sure I like that word." Yet, he knew, he could no longer run away from it and whatever it held in store for him. "But I will abide by this destiny. Because you, Tashina, have deemed it so."

"Be well, beloved, and be happy. Your spirit-brother, Torra, will look after and guide you, he who always has been much more than he seems. When the time is right, you and I and our son will be together again. I promise you." With that, she walked toward him and, holding Hotah in one arm, wrapped the other around Sky Wolf's neck, pressing close.

"Tashina," he whispered, returning her embrace, breathing in her scent, feeling the warmth of her body. Their lips met. He gazed lovingly into the laughing eyes of his son. And then, Tashina and Hotah were gone.

Sky Wolf awoke, his heart soaring.

And knew what he had to do.

In bright morning sunlight, Sky Wolf approached the Demon, the *Kuront*, Renegades. The Lakota bore no weapons. He wore only a loin cloth, hair unbraided, feet bare. He had painted his face black to symbolize the ending of the violence and vengeance against his enemy. He had come alone. Torra reluctantly awaited at the 'thopter, parked a half-mile behind them. Perhaps, Sky Wolf realized, to never be piloted again.

Torra had not protested his staying behind this time. He was not happy with Sky Wolf's decision, though, chuffing and pressing his great body against his human spirit-brother. Sky Wolf promised to return to him but knew such a promise might not be realized. As did Torra.

Now, with sweat running down his face and beading on his body, he stopped and fell to his knees. Revealed in bright sunlight, the Renegade camp was constructed like most of them were. Tenting, temporary structures made of wood, shrub grass, and the skins of animals. Artificial glowlights alit.

Several of the Kuronts approached. One stood over Sky Wolf, possibly their leader. Scaled flesh glinted in the sunlight. He held a long knife-like weapon in one clawed hand.

"You," the Kuront said in halting English. "Life Slayer."

"Yes, and I slay no more. I am here for your judgment, your punishment. I will not ask for forgiveness, for what I have done to your kind cannot be forgiven. Do with me what you will." Tashina had spoken of Sky Wolf's destiny, of how much more he had to do in the world of the living. But he knew upon awakening from the vision, his future would depend on what transpired here, in this spot. His destiny might never be attained, but he couldn't live with the crimes he had committed any more.

The Kuront stared at him, an unreadable expression on his lizard face. Those gathered around him hissed and gestured. A female came to stand alongside the leader. She said something to him in their clicking tongue.

The Kuront raised his weapon.

Sky Wolf lowered his head to receive the killing strike.

In the distance, Torra screamed.

Twenty

Airship *G.A.U. Regalia*
Six Months Later

"It will not be easy, and will take time," Yer'Mon, the Kuront Healer/Shifter, said to Arden. "For my kind as well as yours. Despite everything, the Kuront's true appearance will still evoke fear and hatred in some humans. It is why I have chosen two other Shifters to accompany me on this journey. We will remain in human form. At least for the present."

"I understand, Honored Fem," Arden replied. Indeed, the Kuront had once again adopted the look of Private Thelma Corson, though she wore her own kind's long, sleeveless blue robe. Corson's persona had been created by Yer'Mon's memories of dead human soldiers encountered on the battlefield, all visualized into one by her extraordinary power. It was an incredible ability, one Arden marveled at even now.

He and Yer'Mon stood in the observation lounge of the airship *G.A.U. Regalia*. Like some rich merchant's parlor, the lounge boasted carpeted floors and plush chairs and sofas. Paintings hung on the polished wooden walls; a small chandelier hung from the ceiling.

None of that opulence mattered to Arden as he and the Kuront faced the wall-sized porthole that revealed the stunning panorama far below them. Clouds drifted by, wisps of feathery white curling and roiling. From such a great height, he marveled at birds gliding below the *Regalia*, the sight of the countryside far beneath, crosshatched in grids of brown, green, and blue. Many times, during his wanderings, he had stared at the sky and imagined what shapes the clouds resembled. He often counted the stars at night, wondering what it would be like to soar above the Earth, to walk on the moon itself.

Now he flew within the heavens. For a moment his reflection in the thick window pane startled him. *Is that really me?*

As a volunteer "test subject" for the new, combined efforts of the Tech-Mages, medical doctors, and Indigene shamans, some of his scarring had been completely reversed. Parts of the more severe wounds had been softened, the techniques working just as Chetan had described they might. One of the fingers on his left hand had regenerated, albeit without the nail. Most of the itching had subsided and his brown hair had grown back.

Yer'Mon, in conjunction with the other healing methods, had restored the vision in his left eye and the hearing in his ear. Still, because most of Arden's injuries had been inflicted years before and become so ingrained, even Yer'Mon, like the other Healer at the Kuront compound, couldn't mend him completely. At least, not yet.

I look so different. Kinda like I used to, only older. Hope, of course, ever outspoken and opinionated, approved of his new appearance. "Now you don't have to wear that stupid eyepatch anymore!" she had declared.

He felt better, stronger, more confident than he'd ever been before. He wore clean clothes that fit him, canvas trousers, boots, a long-sleeved, linen shirt. He had developed a taste for berry pie, which, at the thought, made his mouth water. The Kuront symbol of captivity still rested vividly on his neck. He had decided to keep the tattoo, at least for a little while longer, to remind him of his Second Life. That time had proven to be invaluable, more important than he ever could have imagined.

But, most importantly, he had a purpose, a reason to live other than just surviving. He blinked back sudden, unexpected tears.

"Are you well, Honored Friend?" Yer'Mon asked, addressing him by the Kuront form of respect given to an ally.

"Yes," Arden replied. "Better than ever."

A rden had learned of irony, realizing much of his life had been lived with it. After the blue-fire explosion into the human world, after he had been burned so horribly despite his father saving him, after he thought, he *knew*, he would die, the Kuronts found him. Rescued him. Kept him from dying. Healed him as best they could.

Arden thought then it had only been so the aliens could study him. It would be important for the aliens to know their enemy as they sought to overrun the human world. But in the end, they didn't stop him from escaping.

The Kuront peace faction had succeeded once the inter-dimensional portals had been closed, amassing more support to end the war. Many more, besides the Renegade Kuronts, had sickened of fighting and wished to seek another, more peaceful life.

After speaking with Yer'Mon, Arden returned to the airship salon, where he sat on a cushioned divan, its porthole curtains pulled aside. A constant, barely noticeable vibration thrummed through the airship *G.A.U. Regalia*. Arden felt it as he leaned back, though the thrumming wasn't an unpleasant sensation. Corporal Vega had told him after a few trips, he wouldn't even notice it, that it would become second nature. Arden hoped that wouldn't be the case. He wanted to be reminded, even when he closed his eyes, that he was someplace special, that he was flying.

Across the carpeted aisle, Hope lay asleep at his mother's side, Mirrie also dozing. The cushioned couch they rested on surrounded them in a comforting embrace. *No,* he realized. *Not just my mother but our mother.* Mama had adopted Hope. Arden had a sister, one who had shared an experience with him, a grand adventure, unlike any other.

And now he, they, were going home.

Something moved among the clouds below, spectral, glimmering. Arden squinted. A shape, a…a bird? A harpy? No, no, something else. A man-made flyer, some machine of the Tech-Mages. Not another airship; it was much too small.

An ornithopter.

Two passengers sat within, one human and the other…not. Sunlight glinted off the flyer's bright surface, the sharp reflecting causing Arden to turn away. When he looked again, the flyer and those within it were nowhere to be seen.

Memory stirred, causing him to smile.

Twenty-One

Mahoning County, Northern Ohio
Gaia American Union
January 1873, Post-Renewal

To Mirrie Fredrickson's amazement, impossible as it seemed, the giant oak still stood. Some of its bark was fire-charred but most of the tree looked healthy, even after all the intervening years. Bare, snow-covered branches reached toward the cloudless blue sky, swaying in the winter wind.

Another miracle?

A symbol, she thought. *It will always be a reminder, not of loss, but of survival.*

She, Arden, and Hope stood on what was left of the Fredrickson farmstead in Mahoning County. Through a thin dusting of snow, new tree growth along with low-lying shrubs had begun to grow back. Rabbits, birds, deer, and other wildlife had been spotted from the airship, the *G.A.U. Regalia*, which had flown here from Dennison. Now, with the Dimensional Veil gateways resealed, the Earth would reclaim itself here as it had begun in other places. The land long abandoned now displayed resurgent growth everywhere.

Mirrie shivered within her wool coat, but not from the cold. It was a strange, unreal sensation being here again, the place where she and John had made a life, had raised a son. A place gone forever, but now, hopefully, to be resurrected as part of a new beginning.

Just like our lives, Mirrie thought. *Both humans and those Kuronts who abandoned their weapons, and the Renegades who were already sick of war and living apart.*

Mirrie's gaze flickered to the *Regalia* tethered a short distant away. The immense flying craft maintained a floating position several yards above the ground. Members of its crew and three GDC troopers stood at attention below it. Two of the soldiers were Sergeant Hannah Parker and Corporal Emilio Vega, who had volunteered to join this special "mission."

"I kin still see it," Arden said, pointing to the oak. "The energy

95

storms, the blue-fire. Father and I was runnin' back to the house when the cornfield caught fire. I was so afraid. He... Father..."

Arden turned tearfully to Mirrie. "He threw me to the ground 'n covered me with his body. Oh, Mama..."

"Yes, sweetheart," she said softly to her son. Despite having heard Arden's story before, she knew this place would bring that day back strongly for both of them. The courage and determination Arden possessed must surely have come from his father, whose memory still burned fiercely in Mirrie's mind. She was determined to find a way now to honor John and others who'd made the ultimate sacrifices.

Through her own tears, Mirrie marveled how much of her son she could now recognize after the combined medical and shamanistic treatments, despite the years apart and the utterly alien existence he had suffered through. It was incredible he had retained any humanity at all. Yet, here he was, after the GDC debriefings, the tests, the interviews, the counseling, the native curing rites.

The healing affected by the Kuront Shifter/Healer, Yer'Mon.

She wrapped her arms around Arden, his body heaving with sobs. "That sounds like John," she said of her husband, her own voice breaking. "Always thinking of others before himself."

And, sometimes she had to remind herself, it was a Kuront who had allowed Arden to escape from his prison. John's bravery and the *scientist's* final mercy had allowed Arden to live. For, despite his lack of formal education, Arden's intelligence had proven to be acute, his recollections of the Kuront culture and language quite informative. Her son had been instrumental in communicating with Yer'Mon during the Kuront Healer's recuperation and interrogation.

What would have happened if Arden hadn't survived?

Now he and Hope had both expressed interest in returning to the Fort Ottawa refugee camp to open up relations and lines of communication. *Well,* she recalled with amusement, *Arden had expressed interest. Hope had* demanded *it.* Mirrie had agreed to join them and minister to any needing medical help. Besides, she wanted to meet Chetan Atal and Marilyn Kovatel and those others who had sheltered Arden and Hope.

She had read the letter the refugees had written for Arden and knew such so-called outcasts must never again be excluded. They must all work together now to regain their world.

After sweeping away the snow, only the foundation of the Fredrickson house could be found. In the middle of its weedy, stone outline stood Onta Songetay. Dressed in his Ojibwe shaman ceremonial garb, his hair plaited into two long braids, he took the sacred *migiis* shell talismans from his medicine pouch. He and his four long-robed Singers waited for Mirrie and her children so they could begin the Earth-cleansing ceremony. They stood around a ceremonial drum. Yer'Mon and two other Kuronts, in human guise, stood to the side, dressed in their flowing, sleeveless robes. All looked peaceful, unmindful of the cold.

One of the Indigene Singers was an old friend and colleague of Mirrie's, Audra Kingbird, now called Dark Sky Woman. Peace, calm, confidence, and strength radiated from the former nurse. It turned out Audra *had* been praying after the Eelee attack on the train but to a more ancient deity, evoking a more natural, loving doctrine. She had once studied to be a shaman before attending nurses training. Now, after weeks of additional intensive training, apprenticeship, and transformative rituals, she had joined Songetay on his statewide Journey of Purification. Once that was completed, she planned to accompany Yer'Mon to work at the Kuront orientation and living facilities being built. Still helping others.

Dark Sky Woman smiled at Mirrie, her face beaming. Her now much longer hair fell down her back in a single braid. Her robe shimmered with intricate beadwork.

"Miriam, Arden, Hope," Songetay said, smiling as she, her son, and adopted daughter knelt on a richly-embroidered prayer rug. "This is our first stop on this journey of renewal and rebirth."

"It'll work," Mirrie replied. "I know it. With shamans following your example in other states, we'll bring our world back."

"Lieutenant Camden and two others come," Dark Sky Woman said, pointing to the west.

Mirrie turned and rose to her feet. Two figures approached on-foot, a large, white-furred animal walking between them. The ornithopter parked in the distance had been sighted before the airship landed. It was as if its pilot knew what was to transpire here and waited for them. Lieutenant Camden, who had also volunteered for the Journey, had gone ahead to meet with the pilot, nodding knowingly at Mirrie as he left.

Arden voiced what everyone suspected. "Mama," he said, also standing. "It's the hunter Sky Wolf 'n his cougar Torra. I seen 'em earlier from the *Regalia* too."

As Camden, the Lakota and the cougar drew near, it seemed to Mirrie that Sky Wolf looked thinner than she remembered. Though wearing a long, dark poncho over his leggings and tunic-shirt against the cold, his tall frame seemed less imposing. Yet, he acted fit, so maybe his leaner appearance resulted from some ritual he had undergone. Fasting perhaps? He had mentioned smoking a Sacred Pipe the last time they'd seen him.

But it was more than that. The Lakota's long hair had been shorn. She started at the sight of a healed-over wound on the side of his head. One of his ears had been cut off.

Torra broke from Sky Wolf's side. He trotted to the three Kuront, sniffing and rubbing against them. The aliens, in turn, patted the cougar's head and back. They all smiled.

Torra greeted the singers in like fashion, rubbing against Songetay's hip as he walked past. He pressed his muscular flank against Mirrie, and then moved to Hope where he gently butted his head against the girl's shoulder. With a cry of delight, Hope, also bundled up in thick winter garb, wrapped her arms around the cougar's neck. "Hi, Torra!" she cried.

Mirrie squinted as she noticed something peculiar about the cougar besides its color. Unlike the others whose breath could be seen in the cold January air, Torra emitted no such frosty mist. *Interesting,* she thought, momentarily distracted. *I'll have to ask Sky Wolf about that.*

Camden and Sky Wolf acknowledged each other with a nod then clasped forearms. It was evident a mutual respect existed between the two. Camden walked back toward the *Regalia,* once more regarding Mirrie with a touch to the front of his beret.

"Welcome, Brother Sky Wolf," Songetay said. Then, with a glance at the cougar. "And you, Brother Torra."

The Lakota bowed his head in response. Torra chuffed softly.

"We're glad you've come," Miriam added, smiling.

"My thanks," the Indigene replied in a low voice. "Torra and I have been living apart since last you saw me, renouncing our killing profession, communing with the Great Mystery, performing cleansing rites of our own. I had to atone for the knowledge that those Kuronts I hunted and often killed were no Demons, but instead, were ones who had given up fighting. The Renegades were no one's enemy. I have sought them out to seek their judgment, which they gave." He touched his maimed ear. "Not without a price, though still small in comparison to what I did to them."

Mirrie held back a gasp. The Renegades could have killed Sky Wolf but didn't. How ignorant and foolish humans had been to assume all Kuronts were monsters! How many humans would have been so forgiving?

Sky Wolf turned toward Yer'Mon and her contingent, bowing.

Yer'Mon nodded and bowed in return. Sky Wolf continued, "Now, it seems the dream-teachings of *Ptesan-Wi*, the White Buffalo Calf Woman, and my beloved *mitawin* from the Spirit World, have guided Torra and me to this place. To you. We are ready now. I am no longer Sky Wolf but Mahpiya, your servant. I and Torra wish to offer our help."

"Then join us, Brother Mahpiya and Brother Torra," Songetay said. "Not as servants but as equals. There's room for you both here."

A sense of awe overcame Mirrie. A sense of something powerful. Something wonderful. Something life-changing. A circle had been closed and another opened. A new beginning, not only for her, but for all those here and beyond the Fredrickson farmstead, had begun.

"Let us commence," Songetay said.

Per ritual precepts, Mirrie and her children took the sacred *migiis* shells from Songetay' hand and placed them in their mouths. At a gesture from the shaman, Mahpiya knelt beside them and did the same. Torra sat on his haunches, watching. One of the Singers began tapping out a slow rhythm on the drum.

Songetay chanted, his rich tenor giving voice to a Song of Healing. The Singers joined in, their beautiful voices strong and sure, Dark Sky Woman's soaring above the rest. A soft humming arose from the Kuronts, their alien voices accompanying the human chorus. Mirrie Kosanavic, once Nurse Matron for the Gaia Defense Coalition, her fingers entwined with Arden's and Hope's, bowed her head. From the corner of her eye, she saw Hope take Mahpiya's hand.

And then, opening her little mouth, the stone visibly tucked firmly in one cheek, Hope began to sing. Her voice, lilting and confident, blended with the Singers', harmonizing, strengthening. Arden gasped at her side. When Mirrie looked, she saw both him and Mahpiya smiling.

Slowly, comfortingly, Mirrie closed her eyes and embraced the song's rising power and beauty. Its healing message of peace and harmony flowed through her. It was a song of the heart and soul for the Earth and its inhabitants — plant, animal, human, and Kuront alike.

A song of hope, indeed.